LOTTERY OF DEATH . . .

The man he had been following went up some steps and into a house without knocking.

"Damn!" the stalker blurted and turned back to Main Street. Who? He didn't care who it might be this time. Man or woman, he didn't care. The screaming jolted through his mind.

Three women came from a store. Two older ones and a young one.

Yes, any one of them would be fine. The screaming had come again, and he couldn't shut it out—except with blood . . .

DON'T MISS THESE
ALL-ACTION WESTERN SERIES
FROM THE BERKLEY PUBLISHING GROUP

THE GUNSMITH by J. R. Roberts
Clint Adams was a legend among lawmen, outlaws, and ladies. They called him . . . the Gunsmith.

LONGARM by Tabor Evans
The popular long-running series about U.S. Deputy Marshal Long—his life, his loves, his fight for justice.

LONE STAR by Wesley Ellis
The blazing adventures of Jessica Starbuck and the martial arts master, Ki. Over eight million copies in print.

SLOCUM by Jake Logan
Today's longest-running action Western. John Slocum rides a deadly trail of hot blood and cold steel.

◆─► WESLEY ELLIS ◄─◆

LONE STAR

AND THE
RIVER OF NO RETURN

J

JOVE BOOKS, NEW YORK

LONE STAR AND THE RIVER OF NO RETURN

A Jove Book / published by arrangement with
the author

PRINTING HISTORY
Jove edition / November 1993

All rights reserved.
Copyright © 1993 by Jove Publications, Inc.
This book may not be reproduced in whole
or in part, by mimeograph or any other means,
without permission. For information address:
The Berkley Publishing Group,
200 Madison Avenue,
New York, New York 10016.

ISBN: 0-515-11239-9

A JOVE BOOK®
Jove Books are published by The Berkley Publishing Group,
200 Madison Avenue, New York, New York 10016.
JOVE and the "J" design are trademarks belonging to Jove Publications, Inc.

PRINTED IN THE UNITED STATES OF AMERICA

10 9 8 7 6 5 4 3 2 1

★

Chapter 1

A man stripped to the waist lay on the bank of the Salmon River in central Idaho Territory. He had a broken leg with the white bones showing through a bloody wound. An ugly eight-inch-long gash on his belly bled a stream of crimson down his side until it dripped off, soaking into the loose soil. His hands had been tied behind his back, and he sprawled on the grass, staring with pain-dulled eyes at the man standing over him.

"For the love of God, don't do this. I've got a wife and family to support. I still don't know why you hate me so much. I hardly know you. How did I hurt you so bad to make you do this to me?"

The man over him didn't speak. He brought down the red-hot pair of pliers and seared a brand on the other man's forehead until he managed to jerk away screaming in agony. A puff of smoke and the faint odor of burned human flesh tinged the mountain air.

"Why?" the tortured man bellowed once more, then he passed out from the pain of the branding and the broken leg and the bleeding gash in his belly.

The man near the small fire worked faster then. The red-hot pliers that he held with another pair of pliers seared the flesh on the unconscious man's forehead again and again, then he moved the branding to the man's bare chest, the burn marks forming a pattern.

When the man with the pliers finished, he stared down at the broken and dying victim. Blood continued to flow from his belly wound. It would take an hour more for the unconscious man to bleed to death.

The killer took out his bloody knife and swept it across the tortured man's throat, slicing through one carotid artery and his windpipe. Blood spurted six feet from the artery in spastic pulsations as the man's heart continued to pump. The next three spurts soared only five feet, the next eased to three feet, and slowly the spurts grew smaller and smaller, until the blood only oozed from the artery. Within two minutes the bleeding stopped all together.

The killer who stood over the body grunted, stomped out the fire, and shoved the two pair of pliers into his pocket, then turned and walked into the woods.

It was two days later before a fisherman found the body. He looked away quickly but not before his stomach turned over and he threw up. A half hour later the fisherman led Sheriff Mark Kellerman to the spot.

Kellerman was thirty-four years old, single, and stood five eleven, with soft reddish hair tinged a light brown. He was slender and in good shape for his rugged job. Kellerman was a do-it-all sheriff, not the office type.

He bent over the body and shook his head. "What kind of an animal would do this to another human being? Torture, damn!" He waved to his deputy to come up, and the other lawman covered his mouth, but his stomach didn't turn over.

"Mother of God, what is happening in our town?" Deputy Rob Edwards demanded. "That's Zeek Young, works out at the mill. Best sawyer we had in months out there. Zeek never made an enemy in his life. Why the hell has someone done this to Zeek?"

Sheriff Kellerman swore softly to himself. This was the second one, the second murder in Ruggins County in the past month. Hadn't been a killing here in five years. What in hell was going on?

"Look at those burned designs," Sheriff Kellerman said.

"That's the same thing that was burned into Will Stone about a month ago, remember? A circle with a star in it, then those upside down crosses. Is that some kind of satanism?"

"Got me. Don't even know what you mean. I'll go get the undertaker to pick up the body. Think we'll find anything around here to help us?"

"Not likely. Didn't last time. Just a small fire stomped out. Body been here two, maybe three days. No marks in the grass. No horse prints around in the soft ground. The killer didn't drop anything that we can use. Not even a match or a burned out cigar."

"Didn't Will Stone work out at the Starbuck Mill?" the sheriff asked.

"Will Stone . . ." The deputy took off his hat and wiped away a line of sweat. he put the issue wide-brim hat back on carefully then nodded. "Yep, Will was out there, too. Worked the green chain as foreman as I recollect. Good man. We couldn't find anybody in town who thought bad of Will. What's happening here, Sheriff?"

"Wish I knew." Kellerman looked toward the small town of Ruggins, Idaho. "We're what, three miles from town? Far enough away so nobody could hear this poor soul screaming. Them burns was made while he was still alive. We've got a real sadistic bastard running around our town, Rob."

He stood and began a slow search around the grassy bank of the river. "Worst part is he's one of the Starbuck workers. That's two of them dead, so I reckon that I better send Miss Starbuck a letter letting her know. She likes to take care of her people. She won't be a bit pleased about this. I'll make that a telegram. Send it down on the stage to Boise, where they can get it on the telegraph wire."

Sheriff Mark Kellerman wiped his brow and settled his hat back in place. "Damn! Not much more we can do here. You better go bring old Yarnes, the undertaker. I'll look around here until you get back."

Deputy Rob Edwards walked to where he had tied his mount, stepped into his saddle, and rode the roan upriver toward the small town of Ruggins.

Sheriff Kellerman searched the area thoroughly. He dropped to his knees and worked around and around the body. He found nothing to help. Just like last time. He kept up the search, moving grass and weeds aside, feeling every square inch of the ground back ten yards from the body. Nothing. Not a thing that would help him find the killer.

As he searched, he worried how he would word the telegram to Miss Starbuck. She had to know about this.

The Oregon Hotel in Portland was plush and comfortable, but Jessie Starbuck wasn't sure that she wanted to stay much longer. There had been six days of continual rain, and that didn't lighten her spirits. She and Ki had come to this largest Oregon town to handle problems with her Trans-Pacific Shipping Corporation, and all had not gone well. She had had to replace the general manager for inefficiency, but no charges had been leveled against him for fraud or embezzlement. They could have been.

Jessie trusted her handpicked management people, and when one went bad, it hurt her. She let him resign quietly and strongly suggested that he return to the company the more than twenty thousand dollars that was missing. He feigned innocence, but a day later a messenger came with a satchel containing over fifteen thousand in cash and a note indicating that the rest of the money had been spent foolishly.

Jessie waved at Ki, who stood beside the window, watching the rain pelt down on Broadway. The last of the business meetings scheduled had been completed.

"Next we were to go to Seattle?" Jessie asked.

Ki nodded.

"Seattle has as much rain as Portland does. It's not the same as back on the Circle Star ranch in Texas. I'm starting to miss that dry, sunny weather."

Jessie Starbuck was the only daughter of the internationally known Alex Starbuck, a worldwide player in a dozen different industries and one of the world's most prominent entrepreneurs.

His power and money had attracted a diabolical cabal that tried to recruit him to help them gain control of the world's financial markets.

Alex Starbuck refused to join and openly chastised the cabal. The result was that the cartel murdered Alex on his own ranch in Texas several years ago.

Now Jessie tended to the widespread industrial, shipping, ranching, manufacturing, and a hundred other businesses in Starbuck Enterprises. She often had to take trips to different places around the world and within the United States to handle problems.

Jessie stood tall and lissome; she was in her twenties and had jutting breasts, sensuously rounded thighs, and tight, high buttocks. Her hair was a halo of coppery blond that came halfway down her back. Her green eyes in a cameo face and her pert nose gave her a touch of feline audacity, especially her wide-set eyes. Her dimpled chin suggested a shrewish side, but there was a humorous twist to her full lips.

Ki was her half-Japanese, half-American bodyguard and firm right arm, who accompanied her wherever she went. Ki had been raised in Japan by a *ronin*, a master samurai teacher. Ki learned all the martial arts and mystical powers of the samurai and was hired by Alex Starbuck many years ago to be protector of the young, motherless Jessie.

Ki had watched her grow into a tantalizing and beautiful woman, and his task of guarding her had been compounded after her father's death. Ki was a shade under six feet, two inches tall, with a slender, highly muscled body honed and trained in the martial arts. He wore his jet-black hair shoulder length, and a black pencil mustache, and his skin was lightly bronzed by the sun. His dark brown eyes were slanted and almond shaped.

His long years of serving Jessie had built an unbreakable bond between the two that was based on mutual affection and respect.

Ki had considered Jessie his master since her father died. That meant that they could never be lovers. That would make

5

them equals, and that would strip Ki of all his honor. A samurai without honor was no man at all, worse than a dead man, and he would have to kill himself with the traditional *seppuku* suicide ritual of disembowelment.

Jessie looked up as someone rapped on the Portland Hotel suite door. Ki answered it and brought to her a thin yellow envelope.

She took it and without a word tore open the folder and removed the yellow message paper. Jessie read the telegram and handed it to Ki.

It read, "TWO WORKERS AT STARBUCK LUMBER MILL HERE IN RUGGINS, IDAHO TERRITORY MURDERED UNDER SUSPICIOUS CIRCUMSTANCES STOP RITUAL KILLINGS STOP SEEK YOUR INSTRUCTIONS STOP MARK KELLERMAN SHERIFF RUGGINS COUNTY IDAHO TERRITORY STOP"

Ki handed her the telegram, went to a large leather case, and checked through it. He brought back a folder marked, "IDAHO TERRITORY."

Jessica nodded. "Thank you, Ki, you're thinking what I was. I don't remember that particular operation in Idaho."

She worked through the file and soon found the lumber mills. She had four mills, mostly small- to medium-size, along the west border of Idaho. They cut lumber from her timberlands to satisfy the local population.

The mill at Ruggins also cut a lot of red cedar and shipped it by wagon to Boise, where it was used in manufacturing cedar chests.

Jessie read on. The town of Ruggins was small, maybe four hundred people, with sixty men working in her sawmill and lumbering operation. Two of her workers murdered. Why? She thought at once of the widows and children. How could they survive? Split the children up and send them to relatives, and the widow to stay with a sister or brother and never really be a part of the family? Not her workers.

"We better change plans and go to Ruggins. We need to find a stagecoach that will get us as far as Boise."

Ki turned and left the room. He would arrange the best transport to the new problem site.

Jessie had fleeting thoughts of some other project she had in that area, but try as she might, it didn't come to mind. She flipped through the projects in Idaho and soon found it.

Ruggins was on the banks of the main fork of the Salmon River. For years the stream had been called the River of No Return, due to its furious white-water rapids that allowed no boat to work back up the river once it had completed the miracle of floating down the rapids without breaking up.

The Salmon River ran through the center of Idaho, where there were no roads, no trails, where few Indians even lived. There were no outback settlements, no lonesome cabins. It was a primitive wilderness, much the same as it must have been five thousand years ago. The mountains were steep and jagged and covered with conifers and brush that had been compared to a rain forest.

Jessica had been fascinated with the discovery of gold in the Idaho mountains ever since E. D. Pierce made Idaho's first gold strike back in 1860. She had investigated the area and outfitted several prospectors to work in and through the Idaho mountains searching for the elusive yellow metal.

The last push had been to put a team of three prospectors into the central section of Idaho's primitive area. She had a hunch that there was gold in there, if only someone could locate it.

She had three men working up the main trunk of the Salmon River, directly into the wilderness. While she and Ki were in Ruggins, she could also check on her prospecting team and see what kind of progress they were making.

Four days later, Jessie and Ki arrived in Ruggins, Idaho Territory. They took rooms at the Ruggins Inn, an old but pleasantly furnished hotel, which provided Jessie with a suite of two rooms with a connecting door, and the next room for Ki. They had arrived just after noon, and the first order of business was some food. Next, Jessie and Ki went to see

7

Sheriff Kellerman. They had never met.

When Jessie and Ki walked into the sheriff's office in the small county courthouse, he came out of his chair quickly, a smile wreathing his rugged face.

"So, you must be Jessica Starbuck. I'm Sheriff Kellerman. It's good to meet you. I've been here three years, and this is my first chance. I hope the hotel took care of you properly."

Jessie smiled when she saw the sheriff. He was a tall man and she liked that. He had a friendly, kind face that she was sure had been hacked out of a cedar stump somewhere. Jessie smiled to let herself settle down a little. She had reacted with a sudden nervous tension when she first heard him speak.

"Yes, Sheriff Kellerman. Everyone has been most kind. We were in Portland when your wire caught up with us, so we came at once. First I want you to take me to the two widows, so I can make some arrangements with them. Could we do that now?"

Kellerman nodded, called for a buggy, and a few moments later he had driven Jessie and Ki to a small house at the edge of town. It had been painted white, and there was a scattering of flowers around the front door.

"This is the widow Martha Young," Sheriff Kellerman said. "She has three children, ages six to eleven. She's been living with the help of friends since her husband died."

Mrs. Young was in her thirties, worn and tired. Life had not been easy for her. She smiled and nodded at Jessie. She knew who this lady was and was overwhelmed that such a rich, important person had come to see her. Jessie talked with the Widow Young for a half hour, with the men waiting outside. When she left, she assured the widow, that everything would be fine.

"The mill will be sending you a pay envelope for the same wages your husband earned. You'll get that envelope for as long as you need it, or until you remarry. Starbuck Lumber will not let you suffer, Mrs. Young."

They moved on to the home of the next widow, Wanda Stone. She had no children and Wanda had started working in a cafe in town. She was in her early twenties, had a hard glint in her eye, and showed the raw nerves of a widow not quite ready to accept her husband's death.

"Miss Starbuck, nice of you to come, but I don't need no charity," Wanda Stone said.

Jessie smiled. "Mrs. Stone, I like to see a woman who can stand on her own two feet. Charity isn't why I'm here. Your husband worked at my mill for three years. So for the next three years, you'll receive half of his regular pay. I hope that you put it in the bank or invest it as a nest egg. This will come to you even if you remarry. It's a small way of thanking your husband for his good work for the company."

Wanda looked at Jessica for a moment. Disbelief, then surprise, poured over her face. Tears brimmed her eyes, and she rushed up to Jessie and hugged her.

"Thank you, Miss Starbuck. You're a good person. Thank you so much."

Yet despite her gratitude, Jessie thought she detected a tremor of fear in her eyes.

From there, they drove directly back to the courthouse and the sheriff's office. Elrod Grimp, manager of the mill, waited just inside the door. Jessie remembered him, a small man with a big voice and a talent for getting men to work up to their potential. He had only a few strands of brown hair over a prematurely bald head.

They talked a moment, then went into the sheriff's private office. Sheriff Kellerman laid out drawings of the two bodies, showing the marks some hot iron had made.

Jessie stared at the crude designs and shivered. She thought about how the men must have suffered. Why? Who would do such a thing as this?

Jessie looked at the mine manager. "Elrod, did these men make any enemies at work? Was there anything that happened just before they were killed that could result in something like this?"

Elrod Grimp shook his head. "Nothing. I've been over their work records and their personal files a dozen times. There is nothing that I can find or think of that might have caused anyone to hate these men as much as the killer must have."

"Was there anything that would link these two men?" Sheriff Kellerman asked. "Did they work in the same area or with the same people?"

"Not in any way. One of them worked on the green chain, where he had moved up quickly to being the foreman of that operation. Zeek Young was my best sawyer, one of the highest paid jobs in the mill. He set and guided the big saw through the logs, cutting them into the various sizes of boards and timbers."

Jessie stood and paced around the office, fists on her hips, a scowl on her pretty face. "What's left? The only other element I can think of is their habits. Did they drink a lot, run up big gambling debts? Were they unfaithful to their wives?"

The small man from the mill shook his head. "Both were good Mormons. They never touched a drop of coffee let alone alcohol. As far as I know they never gambled or had any affairs with other women. They were good family men."

Jessie shook her head. "What are these symbols that have been branded into the men? Anyone recognize them?"

Jessie stared at the drawings. On each man's chest was a circle with a five-pointed star in it. Beside the circle and on each man's forehead was an upside-down cross.

"Don't these symbols have something to do with devil worship?" Jessie asked.

"I had the same thought, but there's nobody in town who knows anything about such things," Sheriff Kellerman said. "I asked everyone I thought might know after the first killing a month ago."

"So, what we have are two murders, and with absolutely nothing in common between the two men except they worked for the Starbuck Lumber Company," Jessie said. "What that means is the killings must be random. The victims picked out by chance when the killer was in his killing mood. Sheriff, you have any crazy men living in Ruggins?"

"We must have at least one, but I don't have the faintest idea who he could be."

"He," Jessie said. "We've been saying 'he' all the time. Could these killings have been committed by a woman?"

"Could have," Sheriff Kellerman said. "But highly unlikely. One problem would be getting the victim three miles from town. The fire, the branding. It just doesn't sound like woman's work."

Jessica stopped pacing and nodded. "I agree, Sheriff. It must be a man, but we don't have any clues whatever to go on." She walked up to the table where the drawings lay and pounded one of them with her fist. "I don't care how long it takes, I'm not leaving town until we unravel this mystery and punish this killer."

Someone knocked on the sheriff's private office door. He excused himself and opened it, listened a moment, and then walked back near his desk.

"Miss Starbuck, I'm afraid we have some more bad news for you. The men out at the mill say that they have just discovered a body that floated down the river. It became lodged in the gate that lets water into the millpond. Two men have identified the body, and while we can't be certain, it looks like he's Page Dabrowski, one of the prospectors from Starbuck Mining Company."

Chapter 2

When Jessie heard about the body in the Salmon River, her angry frown deepened.

"No, not another one. He was working the feeder creeks ten or fifteen miles upstream on the Salmon River. Sheriff Kellerman, there can't be any tie in between the prospector and the two mill workers. Can there?"

Kellerman moved beside her. He caught one of her hands and led her to a chair. She sank into it.

"Miss Starbuck, I don't see how there could be any connection between the two. We'll have to consider it, but right now I don't see what it would be. Right now we should go down to the undertaker and look at the body. Can you make a positive identification?"

"Yes, I remember Page. He was the leader of the three-man prospecting team. A nicer man you'll never meet." She hesitated, then sighed. "Did they say there were any indications of how Page died?"

"The men at the river said he had three marks they figured must be bullet holes. We'll check to be sure." The sheriff hesitated, his brows lowering over his green eyes. "Miss Starbuck, you don't need to go look at the body now. Maybe you should rest awhile. You've had a hard day."

She straightened where she sat. "No, Sheriff. I want to be sure if the man is Page. If he is, that means the other two prospectors must be in some kind of dire trouble upstream on the Salmon. Is there any road in there yet or even a horse trail?"

"No, Miss Starbuck. We're talking the Salmon River Wilderness Area here, the River of No Return. Only way to get in there is hike, maybe take a pack mule or two, but that slows it down to four miles a day. Nothing but trees and brush, and fallen timber and cliffs and drop-offs and a dozen ways to get lost if you get away from the river more than a hundred feet. It's a true devil of a place."

"But my men penetrated in there. I know of at least three trips they've made in and out, working deeper each time. They must have made something of a trail. They use a pack mule. Sheriff, I still have two men in there. Two men I hope are still alive. I want to find the man who killed my two employees here in town, but right now it looks like two live men should take first call over the two dead ones."

"Yes, I agree," Sheriff Kellerman said. "The body should be at the undertaker's by the time we get there."

Jessie looked at the sheriff. He reached down and she took his hand, and he led her out the door to the street. The undertaker was only a block down. Sheriff Kellerman paused before they went inside. Ki stood behind them watching.

"You don't have to do this. Some of the townspeople knew Page well; they can identify him."

"Sheriff, I've seen dead bodies before. I've even helped some live ones turn into dead ones. Now let's look at the last remains of Page Dabrowski. I know he doesn't have any family in Idaho. I might be able to find a mention of some in my records back in Texas."

They went inside. The room was starkly white, everything painted fresh and clean. In the room behind the entryway, a hunchback bent over a body on the table. It was naked. The hunchback pulled a cloth over the man's crotch and looked up.

"Yarnes, this is Jessica Starbuck. Miss Starbuck, Yarnes, our undertaker."

13

They nodded.

Jessie walked forward and stared down at the remains of the man on the slab of marble. The face had been battered, probably by the rocks in the rapids, but there was enough left that she could be positive it was Page. He had one bullet wound in his forehead, another in his side, and a third in his leg.

"You probe them to see if they are bullet holes?" Sheriff Kellerman asked.

"Yes, that's what they are," Yarnes said. "Probably a .44- or a .45-caliber."

"Would you see that he gets a Christian burial and that he has a stone marker?" Jessie asked. She took two twenty-dollar gold pieces from the pocket in her traveling skirt and handed them to the undertaker. "This should cover it."

The four went back to the street and stood talking.

"Mr. Grimp. I'll be out to the mill about eight in the morning. Some things I want to talk with you about. Oh, pick out two men we can send on short trips tomorrow. I'll see you then."

Elrod Grimp nodded, said he would pick the men, and hurried down the street.

Ki had been fidgeting in the background, and now he came up to Jessie.

"I need some exercise. Been cooped up too long. A ten-mile run will relax me. Don't wait supper for me." He watched Jessie to see if she had any comment that would change his plans. It was his way of asking if it was all right to be gone for a while.

Jessie smiled. "Fine, Ki. Oh, tonight might be a good time to investigate one of your prime sources of information. If there is one available. I'm sure you'll be able to find out."

Ki grinned, turned, and hurried down the street. He had his traveling clothes on: a pair of town pants, a white shirt, a proper vest but no tie, and his ever-present black braided leather headband holding back his shoulder-length black hair. Jessie knew he would change to his loose-fitting black trousers and sandals and discard the shirt and vest before he ran.

14

She turned to the sheriff. "It's almost seven o'clock, Sheriff Kellerman. Could you suggest a place where I might have some supper?" She smiled at him and moved half a step closer. The sudden attraction for this man washed over her like a warm summer sun, and she let the shiver knife down her spine.

Sheriff Kellerman saw her move and caught the smile. His own grin was infectious. "Miss Starbuck, I not only know of the best places to eat in town, I would be pleased if you would be my guest tonight so I can show you some true Idaho hospitality."

Jessica smiled broadly now, her green eyes dancing, the dimple in her chin tucked in delightfully. "Indeed, Mr. Kellerman, I would be honored to be your guest."

They ate at the hotel dining room.

"This is the only decent place to eat in town. Remember this isn't Boise or Dallas or even Portland. We have about four hundred people in town, and most of them eat at home, simply because it costs less. This is a thrifty crowd."

The special of the day was roast beef, a slab an inch thick and big as a dinner plate, with lots of horseradish sauce, sides of vegetables, and a mountain of mashed potatoes and brown gravy.

Jessie ate all of hers. Sheriff Kellerman took care of about half of his dinner. They finished with some newfangled desert made from ice cream and walked out into the faint dusk, even though it was nearly eight-thirty.

"Doesn't get dark up here until about nine o'clock in the summer," the sheriff said.

Jessie caught his arm and pulled it tightly against her side. She felt it rub against her breast and flashed him a smile.

"Mark. May I call you Mark?"

He nodded, watching her with a soft smile.

"Mark, call me Jessie. Now, I was wondering what we could do for the rest of the evening. I have no plans."

The light faded, and soon they walked along the street in the early darkness.

15

"Not much in the way of shows or entertainment here in Ruggins," he said.

"Well then, we'll just have to entertain ourselves." She stopped him and turned until she faced him. Then slowly she lifted on tiptoes and kissed his lips. When their lips parted, she eased down.

"Mark, it isn't often that I take to a man the way I have to you. I really wouldn't mind it at all if you wanted to kiss me again."

He caught her arm and walked her down the street. His voice was husky with emotion when he spoke. "Then you felt it, too, back in my office when we first met. I nearly forgot my name. You are so beautiful, just ravishing, so perfect . . . I'm going to start stammering and stuttering like a schoolboy in a minute."

They turned down a side street, and he leaned against the wall of the store in the darkness, pulled her against him, and found her lips. The kiss was long, and her tongue toyed with his lips a moment, until he opened them.

When the kiss ended, his arms continued to hold her. He kissed her eyes and then nibbled at her lips. "Jessie, I have a house about a block from here. Not fancy, but it's private. I could show you my collection of early American art."

Jessie laughed softly. "Mark, I'd love to see your early American art . . . and anything else you want to show me."

They walked arm in arm in the darkness, down a block, then over half a block, and came up the alley to the back door of the house. Just touching each other became important. For a minute he fumbled with the door because he didn't want to let go of Jessie.

They stepped inside the back porch, and when he closed the door, Jessie went to him in the darkness, finding his mouth, pressing her breasts hard against his chest, feeling his body react and a swelling that pushed against her torso. Jessie broke off the kiss, and a soft sigh and then a moan of pleasure seeped from her lips.

"Let's find some lamps. I want to investigate every inch of you," she said.

16

He took her hand, struck a match on the wall, and led her into the kitchen, where he fired another match and lit a coal-oil lamp. He went out of the kitchen with the lamp and pulled down the blinds in another room, and then came for her.

His bedroom was a man's place. A rifle and a shotgun hung on the wall. A white-tailed deer head with a rack of six points on each side gazed down at Jessie from over the bedroom fireplace. The iron bedframe had once been painted, but now showed two colors. The bed hadn't been made that morning.

Mark flapped the sheet and one quilt back over the other sheet and grinned. "My maid and cleaning lady must not have come today."

"You have another lamp?" Jessie asked.

Mark chuckled, vanished out the door, and brought back two more coal-oil lamps with wicks and glass chimneys. He lit the other two, and the light in the room increased dramatically.

"Better," Jessie said. She walked up to Mark and put her arms around him. "Suddenly I want to touch you, to hold you. What do you suppose that means?"

"I hope it means you want me to kiss you and to touch you." He bent and kissed her lips. She whimpered softly, rubbing her hips against his, finding the hard lump there much larger now.

As they kissed, he eased them down to the bed. They sat there a moment, then he lowered himself backwards until he sprawled on the bed and brought her with him.

Jessie lay full-length on top of his big frame and sighed. "Oh my, but this is nice. I can touch more of you this way." She frowned for a moment, watching his face. "I'm surprised. I don't know what there is about you that attracted me to you. You're handsome and a lawman, that counts for a lot. But that red hair and the funny little way you have of twisting your mouth when you talk—there for a few minutes after we first met I wanted to grab you and take you back to my hotel room."

"Glad you didn't. In a small town people will talk."

"I like this better. You're delicious." She moved up and

kissed his lips, then his eyes, then the tip of his nose. She undid one button on his brown shirt and worked her hand inside, found his man breast, and rubbed it. Jessie caught his hand, pulled it up, and put it over her breast.

She gasped softly as he rubbed her breast through the cloth of her traveling dress. Then he found the buttons and opened three, and his hand went inside and under her chemise and directly onto her bare breast.

"Oh, my, that's wonderful," Jessie said. She rolled away from him, and he turned with her, his hand still on her breast. Then he undid the rest of the buttons on the dress, so it opened to the waist. He spread the cloth and lifted her chemise so he could see her breasts.

"Glorious," he said softly. "Your breasts are perfect, so beautiful, amazing, wonderful."

She sat up and shrugged the dress off her shoulders, then lifted the chemise so her breasts thrust out in all of their slightly pointed glory.

Mark caressed them, working around the pink areolas to the tips of the red and hard, pulsating nipples. She whimpered again, and he bent and kissed both her breasts.

"Oh, yes! Darling Mark, kiss me again and again."

He did, showering her breasts with kisses, rounding each and, when he got to the top, licking her nipples, bringing moans of passion from Jessie Starbuck.

Then she pushed him away. She went to her knees and lifted the dress off over her head, then pulled down two half petticoats and wore only silk bloomers, the short kind that came halfway down her thighs. Jessie sat there watching Mark.

He lay on his back, his shirt open, his hands laced together under his head, smiling at her.

She knelt beside him, swung one breast out so he could kiss it, then straightened and began undressing him. His vest and shirt came first; then she undid his belt and unbuttoned his fly. He helped her pull down his pants and take off his boots. He wore only short underwear.

Together they rolled on the bed, and he came out on top. He bent slowly and kissed her.

"Do that again," Jessie urged. He did. Then he went lower and kissed around her breasts, nibbling at her pulsating nipples. His kisses moved again, trailing down over her flat belly to the edge of her bloomers.

"Oh, my!" Jessie said.

Mark kissed the silk down an inch at a time. When he came to the coppery blond forest of public hairs, he watched her.

Jessie lay there on her back, her eyes closed, panting softly, her hips moving gently in and out.

Mark pulled the bloomers down and off her feet in one swift move, and she whimpered, then opened her eyes and smiled at him.

"You're next," she said. She sat up and pulled at his short underwear until they came off. His manhood sprung up hard and ready. Jessica threw his underwear on the floor, bent, and kissed the throbbing tip of his erection, then lay down directly on top of him and kissed his lips.

"Are you ready?" he asked.

She nodded, with a beautiful smile on her face. "I've never been more ready. I want to stay up here."

Mark nodded, moved one hand down to her muff, and then worked lower to find her treasure. He caressed her nether lips, spreading her juices, then lifted her enough to bring her to the right position. He worked a little higher, then made the connection, and in one quick thrust they were joined.

"Oh, oh, oh! So good. Wonderful." She reached up and kissed his lips, then her hips began a dance, moving around and around. Every two circles, she lifted up and then dropped down on him. Her knees came up to give her more lifting power, and soon she found a rhythm and rode him like a range bull on a year-old heifer.

Her eyes went wide as she dropped down on him all the way, until their pelvic bones ground together. "Oh, my! You touch something that no one else ever has, deep inside me. It's just incredible!"

19

She worked the riding again, built to a gallop, and then her eyes glazed and her breath came in short spurts and gasps and she tore into a series of spasms that shook and rattled her as if the whole world were shaking.

A high keening filled the room as she vocalized her pleasure, then she could only grunt and gasp as a final set of spasms raced through her and dropped her back on top of his hard body, leaving her as limp as last year's Fourth of July banner.

"Oh, my!" Jessie said when she had recovered. Her eyes were bright as she watched him. "Hey, are you still there?" She ground her hips and pumped up and down, using her inside muscles and milked him on every stroke.

Mark's hips moved now. He thrust up to meet her on every move, and soon his own cup ran over. He grunted and panted, and the juices flowed and then jetted out of him as he pounded eight times into her, lifting her tight little bottom two feet off the bed, letting her come down only when the last of the seeds of the race had been planted deep in her vessel.

He heaved a long sigh and wrapped his arms around her, tying her to him.

It was five minutes before he moved. Then he lifted her away and put her on the bed beside him. His arm went around her, and he cuddled her against his shoulder. They still didn't speak.

Another ten minutes and he leaned down and kissed her cheek.

"Starters?" he asked. Her glance came up, and slowly she nodded.

"Yes, that's good for starters. I don't have to be to the mill until eight tomorrow morning."

"Good," Mark said. "We won't have to rush. We'll get up at six and go downtown for breakfast at the cafe where I usually get my home-cooked morning meal."

She frowned for a moment. "This is wonderful, but I can't help but think about those three men who died. It looks like we have a hard problem to solve here, and maybe two problems, not just one. But we'll worry about that tomorrow. I'm hungry.

Do you have any cookies in the house?"

Mark laughed as he stood naked in front of her. "No cookies, but I do have some apple cider that has a little kick to it."

"Oh, yes, applejack. It's been years."

When he came back with the jug and two cups, she sat on the bed hugging her knees to her chest.

"Don't hide them," Mark said.

Jessie grinned, stretched out her legs on the bed, and pushed forward with her chest. He reached down and fondled her big breasts a moment, then bent and kissed each one.

"Mark, you do that about twice more and the applejack will have to wait."

Mark caught her hand and helped her stand, then poured a cup of the hard apple cider for her and one for himself.

"A fire? It gets a bit brisk up here at night."

"How high are we?"

"About thirty-five hundred feet, but there's a breeze that whips down from the Salmon Mountains that has a hint of melting snow in it."

He lit the fire that was already laid in the stone hearth. He had followed the old cold-winter rule of always leaving a fire ready to light in the fireplace when you left a cabin. Some stranger might wander in half-frozen and be able to save himself. It also was cozy in situations like this.

They sat naked on a rug in front of the fire and watched the flames eat into the pine kindling, then burn into the pair of split pine logs. The pitch wood crackled and popped, shooting a dozen sparks onto the blanket. Mark brushed them away.

Jessie leaned against him, and his arm went around her.

"Such marvelous coppery-blond hair," he said. "I love it. And halfway down your back. Once I saw that hair, I was smitten. Then you smiled at me."

She snuggled closer. "When I first saw you, I wasn't sure you were real. I had to catch my breath two or three times. Then you smiled and said hello and shook my hand and our fingers tingled when they touched."

She was quiet for a moment. "I really needed this. I hate it when some of my workers get hurt or killed. Usually there's something to be done so it won't happen again, but now with three of my men deliberately killed and two tortured . . ."

Jessie blinked back tears. He bent and kissed her eyes and held her tighter.

"We'll find them. There's not a chance in hell that they'll get away with this. If they do, I might as well turn in my badge. It's a matter of pride now. I'll do everything I possibly can to run these killers to ground and either hang them or shoot them full of .45-caliber holes."

"Ki and I will help you." She told Mark about Ki, how he was a master samurai and would gladly give his life for his master.

"Ki is quiet and unassuming until he needs to go on the offensive. Then he can battle in ways most white men never think of. I rely heavily on him." She explained how they were not lovers and never could be. "I thought you might be wondering about that."

"I was, and I'm relieved."

The cider in their cups was gone. The fire had burned low. He stood, caught her hand, and lifted her into his arms. It was only three steps to the bed, but she enjoyed the ride.

They lay down beside each other, and the kiss came smoothly, naturally. Then they stared at each other.

"Darling, wonderful Mark Kellerman. How shall we make love this time?"

★

Chapter 3

Promptly at eight the next morning, Jessica met with mill manager, Elrod Grimp. She looked considerably different. She had put on a pair of her favorite cut-down jeans, a white blouse, her low-crowned, straight-brimmed Western hat with a chin strap made from a leather thong, and her cowboy boots.

On her right hip she carried her favorite Colt .38 on a .44 frame in tied-down leather. She had eaten breakfast, changed clothes in her hotel room, and met Ki on the hotel steps at 7:45, and they had walked the quarter mile to the mill site.

Grimp led them to his mill office, well back from the whining of the big saw, and asked them to sit down. Jessica marveled at the raw wood smell of the mill. Douglas fir bark and sawdust and oozing pitch dominated the scene. Inside the office the effect was muted but still there.

Grimp looked at his boss.

"You said to have two men who could take some short trips for you, Miss Starbuck."

"Yes, I'll let you assign them. I want one man to ride north to our three Starbuck mills there and the other man to go south to the mill between here and Boise. At the plants, I want them to give the managers a letter from you asking if anything unusual has taken place lately in their operations.

"I especially want to know if any of the mill workers have been murdered, and if so why. Ask if there were any signs or slogans or symbols around such a body if there was a

23

killing. Once the men have the written statements of these mill managers, they are to ride back to Ruggins and report to you. How long will trips like this take?"

Grimp frowned and peaked his fingers. "The man going south has the quickest, easiest run. He can take the stage both ways. Do it in a day and a half. The one heading north will have to ride horseback up the Salmon River Road. It's more a trail in spots, and it's about forty miles up to the three mills in that area. I'd say it will take that one at least five days. Two days each way and a day there for the answers."

"Tell him to do thirty-five miles a day in the saddle, get the answers from the managers in an hour each, and be back here in three days. No more. We need the information."

Jessie stood and paced to a window that looked out over the mill itself, the mill pond afloat with logs, and a stack of cold deck logs beside the pond that would be used when snow closed down the logging roads and no new sticks could be brought down to the river and thence to the mill.

"Mr. Grimp. We'll be working on finding the killer as fast as we can. At the same time we need to get upstream on the Salmon and see if we can find out what happened to our other two prospectors up that way. I'd like to get moving by noon if we can. Ki, would you locate one pack mule for us, and get minimal camp gear and food for eight days. Make that for three of us. We'll hike up for four days, and if we don't find anything, we'll come back. Oh, tell Sheriff Kellerman of our plans and ask if he wants to come along or send a deputy. This is really lawman work we'll be doing."

Ki nodded and slipped out of the sawmill manager's office.

"Now, Mr. Grimp. There's one more thing I want you to do for me. Two of your workers died. I can only guess that there might be someone out there who has been fired or laid off or quit the mill here in the past year who has a grudge against us. Will you check your records right now and find out who has been fired in the past year?"

"Certainly. I have those records. Let me go get the employee list, and we can work it out quickly."

He came back five minutes later with two big ledger books and a number of file folders.

He opened one of the books and ran his finger down the names on the page.

"Yes, here's the first one, Dub Frenhauser. He was separated from our employment for missing too many days of work. He drank a lot and just didn't care if he worked or not. A month or so after he was fired, he left for Boise. I have no idea where he is now."

"He couldn't be a suspect. Who else?"

"The next man who was let go was Felix Terrill. Had trouble with him since the day he started. He got a girl in trouble here in town, wouldn't marry her, and her father came and the three of us talked about it. Felix agreed I could send half of his wages to the girl. Two days after he agreed to that he left town, and we haven't seen him since. He wasn't actually fired, but he might have some bad feelings about the company and the half salary impoundment for his pregnant girlfriend."

"So he's not much of a suspect either. Any more?"

Grimp took out the second book and opened it to a marked page.

"Yes, I remember this one well, Garth Oberlin. He had worked for me for almost five years here at the mill. He took to drink for breakfast now and then. He'd come late to work, or he'd cause an accident. One of the accidents resulted in a man losing his hand. Garth was prone to accidents. After the sixth one I warned him.

"The accidents just kept on happening. Finally I had to let him go. Paid him a month's wages after he left. Garth still won't speak to me. Crosses the street if he sees me coming. He's still around town, and far as I know, he hasn't found a new job yet. His wife was a schoolteacher here, so they get by. He's not a happy man."

"We'll check him out," Jessie said. "Can you tell me where he lives?"

He did, and she wrote down the address.

"Any more?"

Grimp moved to another marker in the book and nodded.

"Yep, know this one right well, too. Brock Henshaw. He's about forty, I'd say, and probably the smartest man in town. Claims he graduated from Harvard back east somewhere. He's smart, that's for sure. He started the general store here, maybe ten years ago. Things slowed down, so he took a job at the mill and his wife handled the store. I had to fire him for moral reasons."

"Just what do you mean?" Jessie asked. "Did he steal from the company?"

"No, it's personal, Miss Starbuck. I can say that I fired him, and he was furious and yelled and screamed, but after that I haven't heard a word from him. He's busy all day working at the store. Does a good job down there."

"Mr. Grimp, I do need to know the reason that you fired him. It could make a difference in my investigation."

Beads of perspiration popped out on Grimp's balding head. He wiped moisture from his face and took a long breath. When he looked up, there were tears in his eyes.

"This is exceedingly painful, Miss Starbuck. I don't know how to be delicate." He wiped his forehead again. "You must know?"

"Yes."

"Oh, damn. All right. I caught Brock Henshaw having sex with my teenage daughter in my living room. My wife was at a meeting that Sunday afternoon. I'd gone for my usual five-mile walk, but I hurt my ankle and came back early. My daughter said it had happened before and that she teased him into it. She said it wasn't his fault. But I had to fire the man. There was nothing else I could do."

"I understand, Mr. Grimp. Henshaw is still in town?"

"Yes, at the general store."

"Is he bitter about being fired?"

"No, relieved, I'd think. The store is doing nicely now, and it takes both of them to run it."

"But he should still be a suspect in these two killings?"

"I'd think so, yes."

"That's the lot of them, those four?"

"Yes, Miss Starbuck."

"I'll come back and have a tour of your operation later, Mr. Grimp. From my reports, it seems you're doing extremely well here. Right now I need to get ready to go up the Salmon River."

"You're not going in there, too, are you, Miss Starbuck?"

"Of course. I don't ask my people to do anything that I wouldn't. I've been in wilderness areas before—deserts, mountains, and rain forests as well."

She stood and went to the door. "Thank you for being honest with me, Mr. Grimp. We'll get to the bottom of this as quickly as we can. Oh, have you found a new sawyer?"

"Yes, we have two other men who fill in on the job. We're getting along with no slowdown in production."

An hour later, Jessie stood beside Ki and Sheriff Mark Kellerman at the edge of town. They had one sturdy mule loaded down with a modest pair of packs slung across its back and tied down securely.

On top of one of the packs a rifle had been tied; on the other, Ki's short bow and a pack of arrows.

"We can live off the land," Ki said. "But since we're on a quiet mission, we can't use the rifle or our six-guns. With the arrows I can bring down some small game or birds for our dinner."

Sheriff Kellerman nodded. "From time to time there are Indians along the river. They come from the other side of the mountains to find certain berries and nuts, but I'm not sure just what times they come. Probably won't see them. We'll be looking for whoever killed Page." He looked at Jessie.

"It couldn't have been a fight between the three of them, could it?"

Jessie smiled. "No, they were longtime friends, had saved each other's hides more than once, and were more like brothers than rivals. If any one of them makes a find, they all benefit equally." She pointed upstream. "What's it like up there?"

"More trees than you've ever wanted to see. Brush, rocks,

27

a small trail for a while that fishermen use, but then after half a mile, nothing."

"If the mule can make it, I can make it," Jessie said. "Let's get moving."

They wound along the river on a beaten foot trail. Within five minutes they were in a world of towering Douglas fir trees jutting a hundred feet into the sky. On the forest floor back from the river were hundreds of small firs trying to grow tall enough to get more sunshine.

The brush just back from the trail looked impossible to get through. It held birch and willow trees as well as chokecherry bushes and snowberry and the Indian paintbrush.

Mixed in were stands here and there of Western hemlock, spruce, Western larch, and the velvety flat green boughs of red cedar.

Ki took the lead, Jessie led the pack mule, and Mark Kellerman brought up the rear.

When they came to the end of the footpath, Ki stopped and they all looked ahead. The valley carved out by the main fork of the Salmon River at this point was little more than a canyon, with steep walls twenty feet from the water in places. Ahead they could see where the sheer rock walls dropped directly into the water on the far side.

"That's why we're on this side of the Salmon," the sheriff said. "It's possible here, with work, to move up the river. Most people don't think it's worth the effort. Those are the ones who turn back."

Jessie watched the Salmon River's water. Here it was relatively calm for a stretch of about fifty feet. Just ahead it tumbled and sprayed and jetted down over a massive jumble of boulders, splintered and jagged pieces of fallen rock, and two three-foot-thick logs that had floated down this far and been trapped against the barricade.

"That's just a little one," Sheriff Kellerman said. "Wait until we hit the five-and-ten-foot falls in the river and the rocks above and below them. I don't see how any boat can ever get down them, but some do."

They moved ahead again and at once came to a mass of brush and small trees. Ki threaded them through it, picking out the least tangled route. By the time they broke clear of the chokecherry brush, they had scratches on any exposed skin.

They paused a moment beside a stand of quaking aspens. The leaves of the tall trees fluttered in the wind.

For the next stretch, they walked beside the river, where a high water had swept aside the low-growing brush and made a fairly stable path, but soon they came to another puzzle, a spot where a strong wind had slammed down the canyon and blown down more than a dozen trees, toppling them against one another until they lay on the ground next to the river like a tangled web of matchsticks on a gigantic scale, in some places extending twenty feet into the air.

Ki tried one route, but they had to backtrack. The second try also resulted in failure. The third time he skirted the far end of the fall. They had to wade in marsh water ankle-deep but made it through. The mule plodded ahead stoically, doing whatever Jessica asked it to do. She knew well there might come a time when she would have a serious confrontation with the animal.

After two hours of battling upstream, Ki estimated that they had traveled about a half mile through the brush and timber and rocks and windfalls.

"Is it going to be like this all the way up the river?" Jessie asked.

Mark laughed and shook his head. "I've never been more than five miles, but they tell me beyond that the canyon narrows and it really gets rugged."

On advice of the general store salesman, Ki had bought a machete, a long, heavy blade with a handle, and now he used it with almost every step, cutting his way through the brush and small trees, working upstream through what could only be described as a rain forest.

Twice they entered flat areas that looked solid, only to have the grass give way and sink them knee-deep into a sticky marsh. None of it turned out to be quicksand, and in both cases they worked across the murky spot within a few minutes and battled with the brush again.

Ahead, Ki cautioned them to stop and remain quiet. He took his bow and arrows from the pack horse, fitted an arrow into the string, and moved cautiously forward. They heard the *twang* of his bowstring and a garbled bird's call, then silence. Ki came out of the brush a moment later with a fat grouse in his hand. He cleaned off the arrow and put it back in his quiver. This time he fastened his bow over his back.

He looped a leather thong around the bird's neck and slung it over his shoulder.

The small caravan moved upstream again.

Twice they had to cross feeder creeks that emptied into the Salmon down branch canyons and small valleys. Twice they had to wade in water over their knees to find firm footing. The mule slipped once but regained its footing and made it across.

On the other side of the creeks they paused a moment on the bank and eyed the brush and trees ahead.

"You said the prospectors have gone up here at least three times and come back with a pack mule?" Sheriff Kellerman asked.

"That was in my last report," Jessie said.

"I wonder where their mule went through the brush. If we could find their old trail, it would make it easier."

Ki heard the comment and motioned for them to stay where they were. He moved to the left, away from the water, to the side of the valley they were currently in. It was no more than forty yards wide on this side. He came back a few minutes later.

"You were right. There's a trail of sorts over by the side of the valley. It looks easier than what we're doing now."

They found the trail, and it was easier and quicker. The prospectors had evidently been through the area enough to know where they needed to leave the river and where to hug the shoreline.

After that, they made better time. At each creek they came

to and had to cross, Ki worked up and back the waterway for fifty yards, looking for any evidence that it had been tested by the prospectors.

"They would probably just pan some of the bottom sand through here," Jessie said. "If they found no color, they would move on and not leave any indications that they had been here."

For two hours they kept to the semblance of a trail. Ki and his machete improved it as they passed along. They had just crossed another good-size stream and were soaked to the waist, when Ki held up his hand.

They were in a stand of aspens that was clear of brush and open enough for a good camp.

"Be dark in an hour," Ki said. "Best we stop here for the night."

Jessie sank down to the soft forest mulch of pine needles and leaves that had been building up for a hundred years. She gave one big sigh, then stood and went to a spot where she saw some rocks.

"Look here," she called.

It was a stone fire ring. She dug down under a thin covering of pine needles and leaves and found charcoal.

"Somebody else thought this was a good spot for a campsite as well."

She gathered wood, and while Ki laid out the food for the evening meal, she made a fire. She added thick chunks of fir bark that would burn down to a heavy glow of red-hot charcoal, ideal for a small cooking fire. It would retain heat for a long time and not have to be refueled.

Ki took a small fold-up shovel off the pack mule and dug a pit near the fire. It was eighteen inches deep and about that long. He watched the cooking fire, and when the coals were ready, he took the grouse to the river and wet it thoroughly. Then he moved to a dusty area and threw dust and dirt over the bird until it was coated with a thick covering of mud.

At the fire, he scooped out half the coals and put them in the pit. Then he lay the mud-lathered grouse on the coals and covered up the bird with the dirt he had dug out.

"Be ready to eat in an hour," Ki said.

An hour later, Ki used the shovel and dug out the grouse. He lifted it out and carefully pulled the hardened mud off the bird. The mud came away with the skin and the feathers, leaving the cooked bird ready to be cut up and eaten. The rest of the meal was ready as well. They had hard rolls from the store, strawberry jam, and baked potatoes that Ki had also coated with mud and rolled into the coals of the cooking fire. The hot coffee was ready first, boiled over the fire. They were on their second cup by the time the rest of the dinner was done.

They had come with limited camping gear, which meant no tents, no folding chairs or tables. They each had two blankets to ward off the cool nights, and the fire to dry out their clothes.

After the meal, they took turns building up the fire and standing around it to finish drying off their clothes wet in the last crossing.

Darkness dropped on them like a curtain. It had been light, only a little like dusk, and then in what seemed like five seconds, the sunlight was gone behind the mountains and darkness slid in around them.

They had rolled out their blankets before that and now concentrated on the fire.

Jessica had some questions for the sheriff.

"What do you know about Garth Oberlin? He was fired from the mill for causing too many accidents. Is he the sort of man who would hold a grudge and take it out against the mill by killing men who worked there?"

Sheriff Kellerman sat beside the fire feeding small branches and dry twigs into it. He thought about it a moment, then shook his head.

"I don't know him that well. He's still around town. I understand he hasn't taken another job, spends most of his time at home. His wife is the schoolteacher, so they aren't starving. I can see how a man in that situation could stew and fret and let his anger grow until he couldn't control it."

"Maybe we have a suspect then?" Ki asked.

"Maybe," Jessie said. "What hurts is that we don't know for sure the actual date of the last killing. It could have been one of three days from what I understand."

Sheriff Kellerman pushed a bigger stick in the flames. "We know when we found him, but the death date is open. I'd say one of two days would be as close as we could come."

"What about a man named Brock Henshaw?"

"Brock is another matter. He's been around town since it began, I hear. Pillar-of-the-community type, quit the mill, I thought, because he needed to be at the store."

Jessie told him about the mill manager's daughter.

Kellerman snorted. "So she was the one who tripped him up. There for about a year we had more than a dozen stories about little Phyllis Grimp. She was spreading herself around wherever she could, just for the fun of it. Never charged anybody. Somebody said he bet she had been to bed with half the men in town over fourteen. She's married now. Had her son in a 'premature' birth of five months. A true medical oddity. The baby weighed in at eight pounds and ten ounces."

Ki chuckled. "She was messing around with half the town, but this Brock Henshaw got caught. Yes, I could see how he might have some hatred for the girl's father for firing him."

"Maybe we have two suspects," Jessie said. She looked at the black ribbon of river with its faint blush of white water showing downstream. "How far did we get today, any idea?"

Ki frowned for a minute. "After we hit the trail, we made better time. I'd say maybe four miles."

Sheriff Kellerman agreed. "Three-and-a-half or four. I've been this far, but I don't remember this spot. Four is close enough. I know one man in town who said he'd been twenty miles upstream."

No one said anything for a while. Sheriff Kellerman put some more wood on the fire.

"Up at dawn?" Jessie asked. The two men agreed. They lay down and tried to get to sleep. Less than five minutes later a snarling scream slashed through the woods.

Jessie sat bolt upright. She grabbed her .38 Colt and turned toward the noise. It came again, bold and brash, a roaring, mind-numbing screech of fury that sounded like a whole covey of banshees from hell.

★

Chapter 4

Jessie Starbuck listened to the sound a moment longer, then turned to where Sheriff Kellerman had stretched out.

"What in the world is that?" she asked.

A six-gun shot blasted into the eerie stillness, and the roaring screaming sound broke off. Kellerman lowered the weapon and looked at Jessie through the darkness.

"Welcome to mating season for the big cats," Kellerman said. "Cougars we call them up here. North American mountain lion. A hundred and fifty pounds of purring kitty. The *Felis concolor,* also called the catamount, the puma, and the panther. Seldom attack humans, but they get upset when the man smell invades their territory during mating season. Which must be about now."

"I've never heard anything like that sound before," Jessie said. "Eerie, frightening, so vicious, demanding, aggressive."

"Not many cougars in Texas, I don't imagine. They like the high wooded country."

"He's moving away," Ki said. "I heard him before he screamed. He came within thirty feet of us. The fire helped scare him off."

"Show's over," Jessie said. "We better get some sleep. What time is it, Ki?"

"Can't see the stars."

"I can't read my pocket watch. Not dawn yet at least. Good night again."

When Jessie awoke the next time, she smelled bacon. Ki had it frying on an iron skillet over the small cooking fire. Hotcakes quickly followed, and the coffee was boiled and ready.

A half hour after Jessie awoke, they had finished breakfast, packed up the gear, and started upstream. The trip went easily for a half mile, then they came to a small stream and found rocks to cross on so they didn't get soaked this early in the day.

Jessie led the mule. The animal balked suddenly as Jessie jumped to the next rock. The surprise anchor lurched Jessie backward, she slipped on a rock on the bottom, and sat down in a foot of ice-cold snow runoff.

She shrieked, dropped the lead line, and the mule took two sudden steps backward. Jessie heard the crack as the mule's left rear leg broke. The animal went down in the stream, screaming in agony.

Ki was on the scene in ten seconds. His *tanto* flashed out of its scabbard and slashed across the mule's throat. He let the animal's front legs ease into the water, then cut the ropes holding the packs on the mule's back and threw them to the shore.

A moment later the mule's head sank lower, as a flood of crimson stained the creek's water, and then slowly, the animal's head sank under water and it stopped kicking.

Jessie stood, splashed to the far shore, and slumped down on the bank. She wiped tears from her eyes, and pushed her hat off her coppery-blond hair, and shook her head.

"That poor mule. I must have frightened him when I screamed." She took a long breath. "Well, that's the end of our trip up the Salmon River for today, gentlemen. We can't work through this wilderness carrying sixty-pound packs."

Sheriff Kellerman knelt down beside her. Ki stepped out of the water and waited.

"Ki, sort out the supplies. The goods that will keep, put in one sack or pack and we'll suspend it from a tree where the bears can't get to it. Then we'll pack the rest of the gear and head back."

"We can leave our blankets and cooking gear here as well," the sheriff said. "No sense hauling it back to town and then carting it back up here."

Jessie nodded.

When they had sorted out everything, Ki put a small pack of some soft foods in a cloth sack and slung it over his shoulder. He built a cooking fire, fried the rest of the bacon, and made sandwiches of it. He wrapped them up for their midday meal.

A half hour later, they started back down the river toward Ruggins. Jessie was still soaking wet, but she would dry off.

"Next time we bring in two mules so we can count on one getting through," she said. She grinned a bit sheepishly. "Also next time I promise not to fall flat on my fanny in the creek and scare the poor animals."

The trip back without the mule was easier. They followed the shadow of a trail, swinging away from the river when it did and following the water closely at other times.

They had just come through a stand of aspens and turned into a small meadow beside the river when Ki held up his hand for the two behind him to stop. He turned, his finger across his lips, and motioned for them to come forward.

Jessie looked over Ki's shoulder and smiled. A white-tailed doe stood twenty feet from them looking the other way. The wind blew up the river, so she couldn't catch their scent. Beside her, looking straight at them, stood a fawn that still had spots. The small deer couldn't have been more than two weeks old, Jessie figured.

The doe grazed on the young grass; then for no reason they could hear or see, she snapped her head up and looked downstream. She stood rock-still for twenty seconds, then relaxed and nuzzled her fawn.

The beautiful brown doe turned halfway then and licked the small deer on the face. She looked up, directly at them, and saw Jessie move her head. The doe took one bouncing move away from them, then hurried back and pushed the fawn away from the man danger. The fawn didn't understand and tried to nurse, but the doe pushed the small one toward a grove of four-foot-tall Western hemlock fifteen feet away.

The three interlopers stood as still as they could until the doe had her baby in the hemlock cover, then they hiked on through the meadow and back to the brushy trail beside the river.

At noon, Sheriff Kellerman figured they were still a mile from Ruggins. They stopped in the shade near the river and ate their bacon sandwiches and had fresh spring water to drink.

Sheriff Kellerman said he was going to look for some berries he remembered from up in here. When he was out of sight, Ki moved over beside Jessie.

"My primary source of information in small towns was busy last night. A sign on her door said, 'Reserved for all night. Come again.' "

Jessie chuckled. "Business must be good."

"From what I can find out there's no real whorehouse in town. Ruthie is the answer. Some of the guys told me she's bright, about twenty-five or so, sturdily built, and has no visible means of support.

"She's also supposed to know most of the town's secrets from her after-hours party-girl work. One guy told me she was great, but not to believe her climaxes. He said she found out that men like her to make it with them, so she fakes two or three climaxes to get their motors running."

Jessie chuckled. So that was how the professionals did it.

"When are you going to see her?"

"Tonight, unless you have something else for me to do."

"Tonight sounds fine. Our first two suspects don't look the best. I was hoping we could wrap up that killer quickly and get back up the river. No matter what happens on the town killings, we have to get upstream. If our two men are alive up there, we have to go up and blast them free somehow."

The sheriff came back empty-handed, so they continued their hike downstream. Jessie wondered why the trip back always seemed a lot shorter than the trip there.

When they got to Ruggins, they checked at the sheriff's

office, but there were no new bodies, no new evidence. Jessie headed for the hotel for a hot bath and some clean clothes. Two hours later, when she was clean and dressed, she and Ki found the small office marked, "Starbuck Mining." They didn't have a key to fit the old-fashioned long-key lock. Ki stepped back and gave the door a hard kick right beside the latch, and it swung open.

Inside the room, Jessie found a journal noting the trips the three men had made. It went back three years. She read the last entry first. They had made four trips into the main fork of the Salmon, each time working farther upstream. The last report showed they had found evidence of color at the ten-mile mark. Their supplies were running low. They decided to come out and resupply, take an extra mule this time and some six-foot lumber for a sluice box, and see if they had found some worthwhile gold-bearing sand.

Page Dabrowski had kept the journal. He had also made the reports Jessie had received every six months. He noted the other two men's names and the cost of supplies for each trip. The costs were surprisingly low. Jessie decided that Page's years of scrimping and going without while he prospected on his own had ingrained in him the habit of thrift. For him, spending company money was no reason to spend too much.

Jessie wore another pair of her "work" pants, the cut-down men's jeans, a soft blue blouse, and a bright red scarf tied around her throat. Her hat, after a quick cleaning, was back in place, and her right hip held her .38 Colt in brown leather.

She closed the journal and put it back in the desk. "So they made it to the ten-mile creek. That must be where they ran into trouble. Indians?"

"In this area they have mostly Northern Paiutes," Ki said. "I asked some of the locals. The Paiutes live in the west central part of the territory, but probably have been pushed back into the mountains from the broader valleys. They might not be too thrilled to have white men charging into the wilderness area, where they probably have complete control."

"But would Indians use a handgun?" Jessie asked. "Most of

them want a rifle, a long gun for more range and for killing buffalo and deer and moose."

"Good point. So it could have been Indians or whites. Do we know of any settlements back there in the primitive area?"

"I haven't heard of any. I'll ask the sheriff when I see him. Right now, I think it's time you and I go have a heart-to-heart talk with Brock Henshaw, one of our suspects."

"The one caught with the boss's daughter. I'd lots rather go visit the boss's daughter."

Jessie laughed. "Ki, you are insatiable. You'll have to wait for that kind of investigation until tonight when you see Ruthie."

Brock Henshaw was not what Jessie had expected him to be. They walked into the general store and asked for him by name. His wife, a small, thin woman with long hair tied in a bun at the back of her head, eyed them a moment, nodded, and went in back. Henshaw came out with a book in his hands. He stood two inches under six feet, was slender at 160 pounds, and about forty years old. He had black hair in a businessman's close cut, with a carefully trimmed full mustache but no other facial hair.

He held a pair of spectacles in his left hand and the book in his right. His skin was on the sallow side, indicating he didn't get out in the sunshine or the weather much. His features were on the soft side, with a small nose, a thin-lipped mouth, and brown eyes that watched Jessie as if trying to decide if she wore anything under her blouse. He had on town pants, wide suspenders, and a brown shirt.

"Mr. Henderson, I'm Jessie Starbuck, in town to tend to business. This is my associate, Ki. I'm interested in the Salmon River. You know about our company's prospector who was killed upstream. I just wondered what you can tell us about the river and what's up there. Indians, settlers, cattlemen, what?"

Henderson held out his hand. "Miss Starbuck, I've heard a lot about you over the years. It's good to meet you. Why don't you and the gentleman come back to my office, where we can

40

sit down and be more comfortable? I think I have some coffee about ready as well."

She nodded, and he led the way through a door to the back room, where a desk and two chairs had been set up on one side of the stockroom. Two shelves over the desk were lined with books, and another lay open on the desk. There was no sign of ledgers or stock books or other business records.

Henshaw brought another chair, then poured them each a cup of coffee from a pot on a small wood stove. He grinned at them.

"This is indeed an honor. It reminds me of what Alexander Pope said in one of his essays: 'A little learning is a dangerous thing; Drink deep, or taste not the Pierian spring: There shallow draughts intoxicate the brain, And drinking largely sobers us again.' "

He smiled at them. "Pope is one of my favorite authors. He gets to the heart of things so quickly. I have little use for the modern poets. They simply don't seem to have anything of lasting importance to say."

"You must be quite the scholar, Mr. Henshaw," Jessie said.

"Not really. I just like to read. I am critical of what books I get for my reading. But I like to think I have an open mind."

"What do you know about the upper reaches of the Salmon River?"

"Not a lot. Not many people do. Jim Bridger used to know it pretty well. A lot of beaver came out of that area. That's when the plews were worth a fortune. Beaver hats were all the craze in Europe. That time has long since passed.

"The main fork of the Salmon River goes all the way across the territory to a spot not five miles this side of Montana. Almost hits the Bitterroot mountain range. Got the main fork, the north fork, and the east fork, and then the Lemhi that feeds into it. Lots of river, over hundreds of miles, I'd think."

"Have you ever been up the main fork here?"

"Not farther than a big salmon pulled me one day. I'm not the outdoor type, but I do enjoy fishing during the salmon run."

"Do you know if there are any settlers upstream?"

"Just couldn't say, me not being up there."

"I'm wondering if you think that the Paiute could have shot my prospector upriver somewhere?"

"The Paiute? Not this time of year. They stay mostly in the valleys to dig roots and pick berries and shoot enough buffs and elk and moose to make up their pemmican for the winter lodge."

"There's somebody up there, Mr. Henshaw. Page Dabrowski did not shoot himself three times."

"No, miss, I reckon not. Don't know how I can help you on that one. I can only refer you to Shakespeare's lines. In *Twelfth Night* he said: 'I can say little more than I have studied and that question is out of my part.' "

"Well, Mr. Henshaw, I'm afraid it's out of my part, too, but I'm going to have to dig around until I find some answers. If you think of anything that might help me on that upper Salmon River situation, I'd be more than grateful."

Jessie gave him one of her best shy smiles, which usually brought some kind of a reaction from a man. Henshaw simply nodded and stood.

"I'll think on it, Miss Starbuck. Indeed I will."

Jessie remained seated. "Oh, another matter. You've heard about the two men who were tortured and killed here in town. Both of them worked in my mill, and I'm concerned. You talk to a lot of people, see a lot more. Would you have any idea how these killings might have happened? There was some kind of symbol burned into their chests and foreheads, as if they had been branded."

"Just terrible. I was as shocked as everyone else. I've heard nothing, I'm afraid, that might help you. I'll keep my eyes and ears open from now on."

"Good, Mr. Henshaw. I'll talk with you again. I've promised the widows that I'm going to stay in town until I've ridden this damn killer into the ground."

Jessie stood and held out her hand. "Thank you, Mr. Henshaw. It was interesting talking to you. If you hear anything you think might help, you send me a note. I'll be at the hotel."

Henshaw stared at her a moment and shook her hand; then he nodded and led them out of the back room, into the store.

Outside, Ki shook his head. "Hard to believe that Henshaw was caught with his pants around his feet with the mill manager's daughter. He just doesn't seem like the type. If they were playing sex games on the couch, it must have been the darling daughter's idea, and she was the one who got him all excited and undressed him."

"I had the same idea. Of course that doesn't count him out as a candidate to be a vicious torturer and killer."

Ki snorted. "Doesn't count him out, but it puts him way down at the bottom of my suspect list. I hope Ruthie has some better ideas tonight."

"Looking forward to that assignment?"

Ki laughed and nodded. "I always do. Has something to do with my being a man."

Jessie grinned, then sobered. "Before you do your tough work, why don't you find us a pair of pack mules for tomorrow? Get us enough more food to last another two days, four altogether, counting what we have upstream. We'll meet at the general store at eight A.M."

Ki nodded and walked toward the livery stable.

Jessie had her next assignment. She wanted to talk to the other man in town who had been fired by the mill, Garth Oberlin. She had the man's address in her small notebook. His wife taught school, but this was summer, so school was not in session. Jessie hoped Oberlin would be home.

She found the house a block back from Main Street. It needed a coat of paint, and the picket fence around the small yard had several pickets broken off. The fence needed paint worse than the house did.

Jessie knocked on the door. She could hear someone inside. The door moved inward an inch, then swung fully open. The man standing there had not shaved for three days, and his hair

43

was a dirty brownish mop. A tattered long-john top met his stained black pants. He wore no shoes.

Garth Oberlin hiccuped. His hand came up and covered his mouth but couldn't hide a sheepish grin.

"Oh boy. Sorry."

"Are you Garth Oberlin?"

"Yep. How much do I owe you?"

"Nothing. I'm trying to figure out if you're still angry because you were laid off from the Starbuck Lumber Mill a few months ago."

"Me mad? Hell no. Why would I be mad?"

"Then you didn't kill the two mill hands recently, including Zeek Young, the sawyer?"

Oberlin threw back his head and laughed. He stopped a minute, looked down at Jessie, and laughed again. When he quit, he wiped his eyes and pointed to her.

"You must be that Miss Starbuck, woman who owns the mill. Yeah, you're her. Heard you was in town. Mark me off your list, lady. I didn't kill nobody. I don't have the balls to do no killing, let alone torture."

Jessie laughed now and took a step back. "I think you're right about that, Mr. Oberlin. Sorry I bothered you." She turned and was halfway to the street when the Garth Oberlin called to her.

"Hey, you, Miss Rich Pants. Maybe I didn't kill nobody, but I can take right good care of you just anytime you want. You get needing some, you come around."

Garth Oberlin moved his hands, and his pants fell to the floor. He wore nothing under them.

Jessie looked at him a minute. "You really are showing me your shortcomings, aren't you, little man?" She saw the anger flash over his face, but when he tried to take a step forward, his pants tripped him and he fell out the front door and sprawled half-naked on his porch.

Jessie didn't look back. She shook her head and walked toward Main Street. She was sure that she could cross another name off her suspect list.

44

Oberlin was a slob but not a killer. Then there was Brock Henshaw, the Shakespeare-spouting storekeeper who looked about as homicidal as a fly on a glue pot. So where did that leave her? Nowhere, with no good suspect and no way to dredge up one. This was going to be tougher than she had at first figured.

Tomorrow for sure they would hit the trail up the river. She wondered if Mark Kellerman would want to go along. Ten-mile creek, that was as far as the prospecting party had made it on the last trip. They might be beyond that by now. Or the men could still be there.

She and Ki should be able to make it in two days. She headed for the sheriff's office to see if Sheriff Mark Kellerman wanted to come along. For a moment she thought of being with the big man up there in the wilderness, on a carpet of soft leaves under the stars. She shivered and grinned and walked faster toward the sheriff's office.

★

Chapter 5

At the livery, Ki arranged for two pack mules for the next day, then he went to the general store and bought more food supplies for the additional two days of their river trip. He had it stored in a box and said he'd pick it up at seven the next morning.

Then Ki went to the hotel and gave himself a quick scrub down to his waist in the cold water from a pitcher. He applied a touch of bay rum to his face, combed his long dark hair, and put on his headband. With a clean shirt and a pair of town pants, he was ready for a night out.

Ruthie's house sat alone two blocks from the center of town and a half block off Broadway, on Cherry Street. Ki knocked, then walked in. The door opened on a living room that was set up as close to average as any he had seen: a couch, a framed "Home Sweet Home" on the wall, two straight-backed chairs, and a pair of upholstered chairs to one side; a small-patterned wallpaper on the walls and ceiling; a few pictures of family. The floor had been varnished and recently polished. Ki looked up as a woman came in through a door at the far side.

"Yes?"

"Ruthie?"

"You damn well got that right, Chinaman. What the hell do you want?"

"Want to find out if a goddam white girl is cut crossways as old Chinese proverb say." He said it in a high singsong voice, and for a minute Ruthie stared at him in surprise. Then they both broke up laughing.

"I'm not Chinese, I'm half-Japanese, and I hope you're not busy. I have some Far East Oriental techniques to show you."

"Oh, a Japo. Fine with me. I poked every kind of man there is. You want a quick one or a long one?"

"My long one wants a long one," Ki said, and Ruthie broke up laughing again. She was as sturdy as he had heard. She was no more than five feet tall, and almost that wide, with huge breasts, held in somewhat by a white blouse, and a belly almost as big as that bulged over her brown skirt. She wore no shoes.

"Damn, a real Japo. Don't think I've ever whangered one of you guys before. You got ten bucks for an all-night?"

"Indeed I have."

"Good. I'll lock the door and put out my 'Sorry' sign. Two damn nights in a row. Business is picking up."

A few minutes later they sat on the bed in her bedroom. The room was plain, with no whore's trappings, just a bed and wallpaper over the boards and a small rug on the floor.

"This is where I work. Not much, but it's home. You want to show me that tenner first?"

Ki gave her a ten-dollar greenback. She looked at it hard, then folded it and pushed it into the top dresser drawer and came back unbuttoning her blouse. The breasts that surged out were beyond Ki's wildest expectations. He'd been with fat women before, but they had had breasts nothing like these.

Ruthie's hung like huge half watermelons, sagging with their bulk. The areolas were a full three inches wide, and the nipples already the width of his thumb and half that long.

"Hope you like tits, Japo. I specialize in big tits. All you can eat and then some."

Ki took off his shirt, and she crooned, feeling his hairless but muscled chest and flat little belly.

"Oh, damn! You are as tough and hard as a chunk of iron.

47

How in hell do you keep yourself so lean and hard?"

"I work at it. Run every day. How did you grow such huge tits?"

"I eat a lot. Tits grow with the rest of you. I found that out, and I know men like big tits, so I eat a lot. You want to eat some of these?"

She held her breasts up, one overflowing each hand, and he bent and kissed them.

"You want the chocolate one or the vanilla," Ruthie asked. She caught him and pulled him down on the bed. Ki marveled at the size of her breasts even when she lay down. He tugged and pulled at her skirt until it slipped down over her belly and vanished. By that time she had his pants opened and pulled down.

"Oh, my, long and skinny and hard as a telephone pole. I bet you can tickle a lot of girls really deep with this big whanger."

"Been done for a few," Ki said. Now that he looked at her naked, he wondered how in the world he'd ever find the right place when the time came.

Ruthie laughed. "Hey, I know that look you have. Where in hell is it? Don't worry. When it's time, you'll be there. Now, what do you want to know?"

"What do you mean?"

"Look, Japo boy. You come in here with a ten-dollar bill and want a poking, but what you really want is information about the two murders. Everybody in town knows you and Miss Fancy Pants Starbuck are here looking for the killer. Right?"

"Right as thunder in July."

"So what do you want to know?"

"Simple. Who is the killer?"

"Not so simple. Yeah, this is a small town and I hear a lot of dirt, but not all of it. Hell, I miss things. Couple of years ago I was bouncing these two bachelors in my cunnie for months before I found out they went both ways. They were getting into each other once a week like clockwork."

"So, with all this local lowdown, you have any ideas who might be mad enough at the mill to torture and then murder the two men out there?"

"I don't think it happened that way, because somebody hated the mill. My bet is you're chewing on the wrong tit. Don't think that's it at all. More likely some ordinary citizen who goes off his tight little routine now and then and has to butcher somebody.

"I've seen some of them damn close to that. Course the ones I get come see me for their big fling and screech about how cold and standoffish their bitching home-pussy wives are. Something about the same way could happen to some asshole, only with him it would go a lot deeper, and this guy would need to do a bigger crazy thing to get his satisfaction. So he captures a guy, hurts him bad, then when he can't fight anymore, he brands him and then turns off his water permanent with a knife slash across his throat."

"Who in town might be close to that?"

"You want names?"

"That's the only thing I can work with."

"You see if you can do any good with that whanger of yours and I'll think on it. I think best on my hands and knees."

Ruthie rolled over, got on her hands and knees, then dropped her face and shoulders down on a pillow, pushing her rear end up higher.

Ki took a look. "I'll be damned and thrown into a house of virgins and whipped by them for ten years," Ki said. It was there ready and waiting. He got on his knees, lifted more, and slanted into her. Ruthie gave a little squeal and looked over her shoulder.

"Told you, smart prick, that you could find my cunnie. Now, you got a pile driving ass or don't you?"

No preliminaries with Ruthie. The strange position, half-standing, half-crouching, and nailed tightly to the fat woman, spurred Ki's blood to a fast boil. He pounded a dozen times and then exploded, ramming her up on the bed and soon blasting her hips forward. She went flat on the bed with him on top of her.

"Damn, I guess you are good at your work after all. You gonna die and lay up there all night or you want to talk a little business?"

Ki rested a minute, then came away from her and lay on the bed, still panting hard.

"Business?"

"Hell yes! I work for a living. Sometimes what I know is more valuable than a few rolls in the hay. I got me three names for you to check out. The three names are worth fifty bucks to me. They worth that much to you?"

"You give a guarantee?"

"Only on the screwing. The names are educated guesses, come up with after more than ten minutes of hard thinking."

Ki reached for his town pants and took a folded fifty-dollar bill from an inside pocket in the back of the trousers.

"Your names better be worthwhile or I'll come back and take this fifty out in trade."

"They're good. Might not be the right one, but they should hit your killer or come damn close." She snatched the fifty-dollar bill and looked at it, then nodded and slid it into the top drawer of the dresser.

"The first name to check out is Lunt Rockford. He's only in town from time to time. Lives somewhere else now, but he has a permanent hate for half the men in this town. They threw him out once, ten years ago from what I hear. He comes back now and then, but nobody knows where he lives. He causes some pain, buys some things, and leaves. Lunt Rockford."

She looked at him. "You're not writing this down."

"I have a memory like a geisha girl's obi, tight and sure and never letting anything slip out of place. Now, who else?"

"Next man is in town. He's a strange one. Calls himself Count Andre Malenkov. Pretends he's from Russia. He's nothing more than a small-time con man and gambler, but he's got a lot of folks in town fooled. I think he's also a queer, you know, likes to push his jelly stick up little boys' bung holes. He's never once been to see me. I know he can't be getting that much pussy around this town. Might be a good idea to check with the sheriff and the undertaker to see if either of these murdered men had been sexually violated."

"That angle hadn't occurred to either of us. Yes, well worth a try. This Count Malenkov is a phoney?"

"Absolutely. He didn't even know who the czar of Russia was. Now the third man you might have heard of. He also was in town for a while during the time of the first killing. He could have come back for a short visit, long enough to torture and murder Zeek. This gent's name is Chad Bannington."

Ki sat up, surprise washing over his placid face. "Bannington's been here? We know a lot about Chad Bannington. We go way back ten years with him. I hoped he was dead and buried by now."

"Oh, he has been around the country a good deal. Yes, he was in town for three weeks or so, about three weeks ago. He left then and didn't say where he was going."

"Was he a client?"

"Of course. Where else could a famous man go? He's closemouthed that one, hardly saying a word in a half hour. Then all he said was 'Once more.' "

"Where is Bannington now?"

"The devil only knows. No, before you ask me. I don't know anything about the devil worship idea. Those upside-down crosses and the funny symbols. All Greek to me. Now, did you get your money's worth?"

"More than that. Wish you knew where Bannington went. Both Jessie and I have longtime unfinished business with that one."

"He might come back."

"We'll wait and see."

She sat up and rubbed his crotch. "Now that we have that business out of the way, you might as well get the rest of your ten dollars' worth. You promised to show me some geisha tricks and some of those Oriental positions. I want to learn anything new about my trade that I can."

51

"Profession. You're a member of the world's oldest profession."

"Damn right, sweetheart, and don't you ever let your soft little whanger there forget it. Looks like I have my work cut out for me for the rest of the night."

Jessie Starbuck swept into the sheriff's office just before the day desk man was ready to leave for the night. They had only one man on at night unless they had somebody in one of the four jail cells in back.

Sheriff Mark Kellerman sat behind his desk looking at a stack of paper. He glanced up when Jessie walked in and then leapt to his feet.

"Am I ever glad to see you. I'm stuck here with a batch of paperwork I should be doing. But I'd much rather have supper with you."

Jessie pouted just a little. "I'm not sure I want to go out to eat with you again, Sheriff. The last time I did that, you fed me bacon sandwiches." She grinned.

"No bacon sandwiches tonight. I promise."

"I might reconsider. All day I've been thinking of some calf's liver smothered in onions and cooked just right, with mounds of mashed potatoes and bunches of cooked carrots and peas and maybe some parsnips. Any ideas?"

Sheriff Kellerman nodded. "I know just the place."

Jessie laughed. "I thought you might. I saw liver offered last night on the hotel dining room's menu. I hope they don't run out."

They had dinner, two orders of liver and onions, and then walked back through dusk to his small house.

"I shouldn't stay," Jessie said. "I'm paying for that hotel room, and I haven't used it yet."

Mark Kellerman laughed. "Lady, you can afford it. I offer you a soft evening of conversation and a soothing, warming fire in the hearth, maybe a glass or two of wine, even some cheese and crackers and who knows what else."

"The what else is what I'm interested in. Oh, we're going

52

back up the river tomorrow. Do you want to come?"

"I'd love to, but I can't. Too much work to do here. We have a sneak thief we're about to catch, and all this paper to sort through."

"I'll miss you. I was thinking today about how it would be with my bare bottom on a bed of forest mulch and grass and the stars above, and you there with me."

"We'll have to leave that to another day. But we do have the rest of the night. We can fantasize that we're up there in the wilds of the Salmon River with no one for miles around."

"Except that big male cougar screaming his lungs out at us."

"He's just jealous," Sheriff Kellerman said.

It turned out to be a deliriously satisfying night for both of them.

That same evening, about midnight, a shadowy figure blended in with the darkness just down the alley from the Salmon Saloon. The man was dressed all in black and had a whiskey bottle in one hand. Now and then he lifted it to his lips and drank. The bottle was still three-quarters full.

Two men came down the boardwalk, dropped off into the dirt of the alley opening, then stepped up to the boardwalk on the other side of the alley. The drinker in the dark made no move toward them. He watched, took another pull on the bottle, and settled against the rough lumber of the building.

A man came out of the saloon. He was a staggering drunk. He took a few steps, and the man in the alley came alert. He shoved the bottle into a pocket of his dark overcoat and edged closer to the boardwalk, where the bottle dropped into the alley.

Two steps from the alley the drunk laughed, waved at some imaginary person, and jolted against the wall of the general store as he pitched to the boardwalk and passed out.

The figure in black snorted and backed farther into the darkness of the alley. That wouldn't do at all, not at all. He watched as another man left the only saloon in town and walked down the street. He was taking elaborate pains to walk erect and not stagger, to prove that he was not drunk.

The man in black smiled. The best kind, figured he could handle himself and not lose it. Just the right one. The man walked across the alley, stepped carefully onto the boardwalk on the far side, and moved down the street.

The black-coated figure hurried across the alley, stepped silently onto the boardwalk, and ambled along after him. The pursuer let his victim stay ten steps ahead. When the drunk slowed to look in a store window, the stalker slowed. When the other man hurried across a street, the man in black hurried behind him.

The tipsy man never did look behind. He was confident he was walking like a normal person. Who could fault him, he must have thought. The stalker had figured this out in a flash of recognition, and when the man entered the middle of the first block north of Main, he moved up closer.

The block was dark. Lights showed in only one of the four houses on the stretch. Now was the time. The stalker increased his pace and had come within six feet of the victim when he turned sharply, stumbled against a gate post, and cursed softly. A moment later, the drunk slipped through the gate and walked up the steps to the second house, where the lights were still on. He opened the door and hurried into the house.

The stalker turned and wandered back to Main Street and then to the first alley. He was a block from the saloon now. Too far away. He glanced up at the full moon in the cloudless sky. Maybe tonight wasn't the best time. It had been a last-minute decision to come. He tipped the bottle and drank. Maybe just the bottle would be enough tonight. Maybe.

If not, he could come back later. There would be men leaving the saloon for two hours yet. There was always somebody getting home late after a drinking bout.

He drank from the bottle once more. Things were getting fuzzy. He blinked, then rubbed his eyes. He better get on home. Yes. Tonight was not a good time. Some other night the incessant screaming would come again, and he would listen to it. The sound that blasted him from his house. When the screaming came the next time, another man would die. He felt in his pocket for the matches, the small jar of coal oil, and the two pairs of pliers. Yes, the pliers had worked perfectly.

Another night would be better. The stalker turned for his house. It wasn't far away.

Jessie came awake at five A.M., slid out of Mark Kellerman's bed and dressed, kissed Mark good-bye, and hurried back to the hotel. She had to get into a fresh pair of jeans and a long-sleeved cotton flannel shirt to protect her arms during the hike upriver. They would be leaving shortly after eight A.M. She didn't want to be late. For just a moment she thought about the wonderful night with Mark Kellerman. Yes! Then she put that out of her mind. She had to concentrate on today, on the trip up the river to find the other two men in her prospector group.

★

Chapter 6

At the general store, Jessie found Ki waiting for her. He had all the goods packed on one of the mules, which still made a light load.

Jessie grinned at Ki and nodded. "You're right, we don't need two pack mules. We'll drop off one as we go past the livery."

The second trip up the Salmon went easier. They knew where the trail of sorts was and made good time. Before noon they came to the four-mile mark where they had camped, and an hour later they were at the spot where they had left their supplies. They were intact, still slung in the canvas bag twenty feet in the air. Ki tied his *tanto* to a pole and cut the leather thongs holding the goods in the air. They fell and he caught them, then put the additional sack on the mule, and they moved upward.

Jessie reveled in the pristine woodland. Towering Douglas firs that must have been a hundred and fifty feet tall. Some of them had to be six feet in diameter at the ground. All around were the other trees and brush and lower growth, the aspens quaking with the least little bit of breeze. The Western hemlock and the red cedar were her favorites.

Now and then they came to a growth of birch trees, with their nearly white bark standing out in the shadows of the deep timber. Ki led the way, but now he suddenly stopped.

He shouted out a warning to Jessie as just ahead of them some animal bellowed out a call of anger and charged.

Jessie jumped to one side of the mule so she could see the problem. The mule looked up and bolted away from her, into the brush. Jessie had time only to see a huge animal bearing down on her. She dove to the side and rolled behind a tree just as the two-thousand-pound bull moose charged through the space she had occupied.

Jessie saw the moose as it continued its run for another fifty feet. Then it turned and stared at them and pawed the ground.

The huge rack of antlers with webbing seemed too heavy for the beast to hold up. But he not only held them up, he also shook them at the intruders.

Jessie sat up and pulled her .38 revolver, to scare him away if he charged again. The big animal was downwind of them now. His eyesight wasn't the best, but his nose was perfect. He caught the first touch, then the confirming terrifying scent of man, and he bellowed again, turned, and trotted off into the brush with all the dignity of a general inspecting his troops.

"I'll never eat another moose steak as long as I live," Jessie said. She stood and shook her head. "He was the most magnificent beast I've ever seen. Buffalo are meaner, I guess, but that moose was simply glorious. That rack of horns with the heavy webbing. Beautiful."

Ki pushed a pair of *shuriken* stars back into their compartment in the top of his jeans. He had been ready to use the deadly eight-pointed throwing stars if the animal attacked. He could have killed the moose with a throat hit if he had needed to.

Ki lifted his thin brows and nodded. "Yes, I agree. At least we won't have any moose steaks for supper."

At the next small stream that came into the Salmon, they found evidence of shovel work in the sand along the shore. There were piles of sand at one spot and boot prints around it.

Ki knelt near the spot and lifted a handful of sand from the bottom of the small stream. He used both hands like a gold pan

57

and let the current wash away the light sand and rocks. When he finished, he had half a dozen gleaming specks of gold dust. He showed Jessie.

"Yes, they must be finding some traces, but not enough to do any serious panning. Maybe the next stream."

They stopped a short way higher on the Salmon, in a grove of birch and aspens, and had their noon meal. Ki had brought along a loaf of bread from the store and a foot-long cured hard sausage. He sliced it and made sandwiches, started a small cooking fire, and soon had coffee boiling.

"What do you expect to find up here?" Ki asked as they ate.

"More evidence of prospecting, maybe that sluice box they wanted to build. I'm not sure. We might even find two more bodies shot to death. One way or the other we have to know. If they're up here, we'll find them. Then figure out what to do."

A chipmunk darted from a nearby Douglas fir and stood up on its hind legs staring at them. Ki tossed a bit of bread at the six-inch-long animal with an eight-inch tail. The chipmunk fled in terror, only to reappear a moment later, eyes inquisitive, its little black nose quivering.

The tiny brown striped rodent spotted the bread and darted to it, nose working overtime. He caught the bread with both front feet and stood and nibbled at it in a test. His dark eyes stared at Ki, who was eight feet away.

Satisfied that the bread was good to eat, the chipmunk stayed in his standing position until he had finished eating it. Then he dropped down and ran forward a foot before turning around, darting to the fir, and scampering six feet up the trunk. A moment later he worked around the trunk and stared at them.

Ki tossed another bit of bread but this time closer to them. The chipmunk ran down the fir headfirst, jumped to the ground, and raced to the piece of bread.

"At this rate he'll eat more of that sandwich than you will," Jessie said. Her voice threw the chipmunk into a panic. He grabbed the food in his mouth and raced back to the fir tree.

"He's not used to hearing voices," Ki said softly. The small squirrel didn't return, and they packed up and continued along the Salmon River.

The next feeder creek revealed nothing. They had agreed at the start to work only the creeks entering the Salmon from this side. The river itself was brim-full with runoff and much too swift and deep to ford. They wouldn't risk a swim across with the mule and their provisions, and they didn't want to split their forces, so they decided to stay on this side.

The second creek up from their lunch stop proved more productive. They found shoveled sand and half-buried in it a prospector's pan that looked as if a mule had stepped in the middle of it and smashed a hole right through the metal. Not much use for panning gold with a hole that size.

"So the men were here and worked this area," Jessie said. "But was that before or after they were attacked by someone or something and Page got himself killed and dumped in the river?"

Ki shook his head and they moved on upstream.

The next creek was larger. They got wet well above their knees crossing it. On the far shore they saw signs that the prospectors had worked this tributary as well.

Ki found the freshly sawed-off end of a one-by-eight piece of lumber. The top of it was whitened by the sun, but the underside was still a raw lumber shade of light yellow.

"So they were here recently and maybe built their sluice box here," Jessie said. Ki pointed to where the box could have been set in the flow of the water. Little stone platforms had been built at two places almost exactly eight feet apart.

Ki tried the hand-panning process, and this time showed twice as much gold as he had found before.

"They must have decided the traces here weren't good enough for an operation, or that they might point to a mother lode upstream."

They moved upstream again on the River of No Return.

59

The waterway turned left here and created on their side a fifty-foot-wide beach of soft sand and rocks. The valley widened and was more than a half mile across. For a change, the mighty Salmon settled down and ran almost as smooth as a lake, with no rapids or white water for what looked like a half mile upstream.

The first small stream that came out of the valley held no hope for the seekers. The second one was waist-deep as they crossed, and on the far side they saw a small tent that had been half blown down, a fire ring, and a tarp that could hold supplies.

Jessie fisted her revolver as they approached the camp. Someone had stayed here. The tent looked as if the wind had whipped out two of the tie-down stakes. There were signs of horse droppings near some aspens.

No one was there. Jessie went to the fire ring. The ashes were cold, and it looked as if it had rained since the fire had been used.

From the grove of trees, Ki called. Jessie went over, and Ki pointed to a spot on the ground under the white-barked birch.

"Blood," Ki said. "Somebody bled a lot here, and the blood soaked into the ground. Here, there's blood on these leaves of grass, and more over this way."

"Indians?" Jessie asked.

"No way of knowing. The mule is gone. A lot of its tracks around. But I don't see any unshod hoofprints. I'm not sure if the Paiutes even use horses. Not much value in terrain like this."

"Let's check to see if anything can be identified as having been with our three men. Names, letters, anything like that."

They went through the meager leavings. They found a pack with a clean pair of jeans and a shirt and a straight razor. In the foodstuffs canvas there were only some stale flour, a piece of cured ham, and some rancid bacon.

"Whoever hurt these men must have taken them and everything of value, including the mule," Jessie decided.

"Let's move on upstream. We know for certain they didn't strike cross-country through this heavy brush and timber."

Two creeks later, they had found nothing, and the sun was rimming the ridge to the west.

Ki picked out a camping spot in some fir and hemlock. The ground was soft from a hundred years of pine needles and leaves creating a natural forest mulch, slowly degrading into topsoil.

Ki had moved back from the river to a solid wall of granite that grew out of the land and provided perfect protection from their rear. Jessie dug away the mulch and found rocks to make a small fire ring.

They ate well that night. Ki had brought slices of cured ham which he browned in the big cast-iron skillet. He baked the potatoes in a coating of mud in the coals and boiled coffee while the potatoes cooked.

As he waited on the cooking, Ki worked for several minutes with a pole he cut and some string; then he went to the river and whipped out onto the stream a fishing hook with some fuzzy bits of yarn on it.

He cast the lightweight fishing line out and let the fuzzy hook float down the stream, with the current, then worked it slowly back against the flow.

On the second cast, he caught a trout, a ten-incher. He promptly unhooked it, pushed a sharp stick through its gills, and dropped it on the grass.

When he had three trout, he stopped fishing, cleaned them, and cut off the heads and tails, then moved the ham slices from the frying pan and dropped in the three trout.

"Fish cook quickly," Ki said.

By the time the baked potatoes were done, so were the trout, and the supper turned into a feast. Ki stripped the backbones from the trout before he served them.

Darkness dropped around them suddenly like an enveloping blanket. Jessie moved to where she could look through the canopy of evergreen branches above and see the stars. There were a million of them out tonight.

Jessie pointed. "Ki, have you ever wondered about the stars? Even the ancients worried about them. They're still a mystery. Why are they way out there and we're down here? Are there any more earths out there anywhere? I wonder if man will ever fly like a bird and reach the moon or one of those faroff stars?"

Ki shook his head. "I wouldn't want to go to a star. I'm told those stars are suns like our own. Our earth is a small planet circling a minor star in a second-rate galaxy on the outskirts of the universe. Therefore, of what value is mere mankind?"

Jessie stared at Ki. "I didn't know you were an astronomer and a philosopher."

"Master, I have many talents of which you know little. I draw upon them when I need them."

Jessie grinned. He almost never called her Master, although in a weak moment he had admitted that when her father died, he considered her to be his master.

"Ki, you are a true friend and companion. Always ready when I need you. Do you think we're getting closer to the ones who bushwhacked our team of prospectors and killed Page Dabrowski?"

"Precognition is not one of my talents. I wish I had that power. If our snarling cougar isn't disturbed, we should have a quiet night and can learn more about the missing men tomorrow."

"Knowing the future certainly would be a big help right now, Ki. But like other mortals, we'll just have to let it play out for us. Feet to the fire?"

They stretched out their blankets. Ki made certain that the mule was securely tied to a friendly tree, and then he built up the fire.

"Even if our romantic cougar is out there tonight," he said, "the fire will convince him not to bother us. I'll wake during the night and put on some more fuel."

Jessica stood at the fire, turning slowly to warm all sides of her in the crisp night mountain air. They had been climbing ever since they left Ruggins. She had no idea how much higher they were here, but the air did seem to have more of a nip in it tonight.

"Maybe we'll find them tomorrow. What we saw today must mean that they were attacked and Page killed here and the other two taken captive. But by whom? Indians? There doesn't seem to be anybody else up in this wilderness."

Ki added more logs to the fire, then sat down on his blanket across from the blaze. "Tomorrow we should find out. I figure we're almost at the ten-mile creek mentioned in the journal. Maybe at the ten-mile creek we'll know."

Jessie sat down, put her .38 Colt near at hand, and rolled up in the blanket. She kept her right hand outside, within reach of the .38. She wanted to be ready just in case that big male cougar decided to brave the fire.

With first light, both of them were up. Jessie washed her face at the edge of the small stream and Ki rebuilt the fire. It had gone out during the night. He made a fire of fir bark and soon had a bed of hot glowing coals for his cooking.

He took a small jar from the food pack, unscrewed the top, and poured six already cracked eggs into his big frying pan. It had been greased with six strips of fried bacon, and soon they feasted on scrambled eggs, toast and jam, bacon, and hot coffee.

"I may have you take over the kitchen back at the Circle Star ranch," Jessie said, a faint tease in her voice.

Ki shook his head. "I only cook on special occasions," he said. Then he saw her grin. "Or when I get really hungry." They both laughed.

An hour later, they had moved across three small feeder streams. The Salmon River was a monster here. They found a dozen rapids in the first mile. The water turned white and then light green as it plunged and crashed down four- and eight-foot rock barricades and pounded through narrow passageways in what once must have been solid basalt or granite.

Ki stood watching the water thundering along at what must

have been twice as fast as a horse could gallop.

"Power," Ki said. "The water has so much power I don't see how any boat could make it through this one-mile stretch."

"Let's hope we don't have to try it," Jessie said.

At the next small creek, they found evidence of digging. They left their mule and packs at the edge of the creek and worked up the bank a hundred yards. They found more digging, but no campsite, nothing that looked like the prospectors had stayed long here.

From behind them came a shrill cry, then a scream of terror and agony.

"The mule!" Ki said. He turned and raced through the woods along the stream. Jessie couldn't keep up with him. She ran as fast as she could and burst out of the brush at the opening near the Salmon River.

The mule lay on its side, one foot making a feeble kick. It screamed again, then its head dropped and it was still. Jessie looked around but didn't see Ki.

He came back a moment later along the Salmon from upstream.

"I lost them," he said. "I just saw flashes of them, but they looked like Indians. No chance to use my stars. Is the mule dead?"

"I think so."

They checked. Its throat had been sliced open from side to side, and a great quantity of blood drenched the ground near the animal.

Jessie stared at their packs. Both had been broken open. Half of the food was gone or ruined in a small backwater of the river.

Ki looked over the packs. He untied them from the mule.

"At least this time I got packs that also have shoulder straps on them. I can put what food we have left in one pack. I'll carry it. Now, do we go forward or turn back?"

"We didn't get to the ten-mile creek," Jessie said. "I was counting on it." Ki stared at the food.

"We can make it. It shouldn't be more than a mile at the

64

most. If we run short on food, we can shoot some game. No sense in trying to hide now."

"Look," Jessie said, pointing to something on the ground ten feet in front of the dead mule.

Ki picked the item up and brought it back.

"An Indian arrow. It's been broken in half and placed on the trail."

"That's an Indian sign for saying, 'Don't come up this trail any farther,'" Jessie said. "That was the meaning for the Comanches, so I'd think the same thing would apply here with the Paiute."

"Paiutes, we don't know much about them," Ki said. He took a .45-caliber six-gun from one of the packs and pushed it into his belt. "Not that I'll use it. I just don't want these Indians to think that I'm unarmed."

Jessie walked around the area to see if she could find anything else. She almost missed it. The whole thing was brown and tan and strung on a piece of rawhide. It was an Indian medicine bag of some kind. She picked it up and took it to Ki.

He examined it and frowned. "Yes, a medicine bag. No Indian worth his war paint would lose one of these. Then they have to go through a long ritual to make another one. Maybe somebody in town can figure it."

After repacking the food and camp gear in one of the shoulder packs, they moved upstream. Jessie went first now, her hand near her Colt. They found two more creeks, then what had to be the ten-mile creek. It had been worked extensively. Piles of sand and gravel disrupted the normally smooth slope on the near shore of the ten-foot-wide creek.

They found drag marks where a sluice box could have been set and then moved. To one side under some birch they found where a camp had been made and a fire ring set. Ki looked at the horse droppings and came back with a report.

"They stayed here for three or four days it looks like from the number of droppings. This could have been before they were attacked at the creek below."

"They could have penetrated this far, then turned back and stopped at the creek below for one last workup before they headed in for new supplies."

Ki did his palm gold panning and came up with about the same traces he had found before.

"Not worth working," he said.

"I hate to, but looks like we better turn back downstream," Jessie said. "We must be getting close to something or they wouldn't have tried to stop us this way."

They headed downstream. They had gone less than a quarter of a mile when Ki stopped along the side of the Salmon and pointed across the rushing water.

A large brown bear stood in the river up to his belly. He didn't move. One large paw hung in the air just out of the water. Then in a move hard to follow, the bear's paw darted into the water and, in one swing, swept a two-foot salmon out of the water and threw it onshore ten feet away.

The big bear sauntered over to where the salmon flopped on the grass in a desperate effort to get back to the water. The bear caught the fish by the midsection with his mouth and took out a huge circular bite. The bear sat down, munching contentedly on the salmon as one big paw held down the still flopping fish.

"If I was that good, we would have salmon for supper," Ki said. "I'll try my fishing lure this afternoon when the salmon get hungry and the bugs and insects come out and fall onto the water."

At about four o'clock, by Jessie's ladies' pocket Waterbury, they stopped and made camp and Ki went fishing. In half an hour he returned with a eighteen-inch salmon. He filleted it and baked it in the skillet. It was the best meal they had on the trip.

After a day and a half more of steady hiking, they came out at Ruggins. Jessie had a long hot bath and a big dinner and went to bed.

Ki went to talk with Sheriff Kellerman and showed him the broken arrow and the small medicine bag they had found.

66

"I'd say Paiute," Kellerman said. "Can't be sure. We don't see them around here often. They shy away from our little town, thank God. I guess that means there are at least some Paiutes up in that area."

Something bothered Ki about the men he had chased up the river. They had loincloths and Indian weapons; their hair was black, and they appeared to be Indians. But he didn't get that good a look at them. Something didn't seem just right about them, but if he couldn't figure it out, he couldn't say anything. He scowled, and went back to the hotel.

Maybe a good night's sleep would help him remember what had bothered him up there on the River of No Return.

Chapter 7

A man in bed with a sagging mattress rolled over twice, then kicked out of the sheet and sat on the side of the bed. His wife awoke and looked over at him in the dim light.

"Can't sleep again?" she asked.

"Can't get to sleep. I better take a walk. That usually gets me into a sleeping mood."

He dressed, told his wife he'd be back in an hour, and went out of the back door. He slipped out the back of the eight-room house and walked to the small shed where he kept a horse. Under the end of the feed bin, he moved a board and took out a flask which he slipped in the pocket of his long black coat.

At the edge of the shed he opened the flask and drank deeply from the amber fluid. He gasped as the whiskey went down. He coughed once, then nodded.

"Oh, yes. Now, that's better. Those damn voices won't come now!"

He pushed the flask into his pocket and walked toward the center of town. In the middle of each block, he took out the flask in the darkness and drank. But still the voices screamed at him. Setting his brain on fire. Halfway down the next block, a dog began to bark. He eased up to the side of the dark house and waited for the dog to come around the corner again. When it did, the man kicked the medium-sized animal in the head, toppling it over. It lay there stunned.

A knife flashed in the soft light of the half moon, then bright red fluid spurted from the dog's throat, drained out in a crimson flood. The man wiped the knife blade off on the white fur of the animal, put the weapon back in his pocket, and continued his walk.

The screaming sounded in his head again. He couldn't stop it. There was only one way to stop the screaming. The dog's blood had not been enough. He drank again. By the time he got to Main Street, the bottle was empty. He threw it down an alley and heard it shatter on some stones.

He laughed. The screaming came to him again, and he held his hands over his ears but couldn't stop it. A man left a store ahead of him, and the man in the long black coat followed him.

The man ahead paused at a store window and looked in. The place was closed. He wandered on, and the stalker decided the man must be a salesman killing time. That reminded him of something his father always told him: The best way to kill time is to work it to death.

The salesman turned down a side street, and the stalker hurried and ran around the corner. He couldn't see the man he had been following. Then he emerged from a shadow half a block ahead and went up some steps and into a house without knocking.

"Damn!" the stalker blurted and turned back to Main Street. Who? He didn't care who it might be this time. Man or woman, he didn't care. The screaming jolted through his mind, and he held his head and leaned against the wall of a building.

Just down the block, three women came from a store. They had been taking an inventory. They walked together toward him. He vanished down the blackness of an alley and watched them go by. Two older ones and a young one.

Yes, any of them would be fine.

He had to do it tonight. The screaming had come again, and he couldn't shut it out—except with blood. The dog's blood hadn't worked. He followed the three women half a block behind. Two of them went to one house and waited until the third woman walked inside, lit a lamp, and waved at them out the door. He could hear the door lock all the way on the street.

Half a block later the two women went up to another house and inside without knocking.

Now, when the last woman came out to walk home, he'd have his victim. How else could she get home? Yes. He grinned, wishing he had another drink. The church didn't approve of drinking. He'd kept his hidden for thirty years. That should be long enough.

The man in the black overcoat watched in surprise and anger as the last woman of the three came out of the house. Right behind her walked a large man, well over six feet tall. The stalker recognized the man now, the woman's husband. He had been playing cards or something at a friend's house while the women worked. Damn! No chance there.

He turned away and headed back to Main Street. A heavy drinker would be his best bet. The voices screamed in his head, and he turned and ran the other way. He ran for fifteen minutes, not caring where he went. Ran until he couldn't go a step farther. Until his own blood pounding in his head drowned out the raucous screams. He dropped to his knees and panted. His lungs burned, and his breath came in gasping gulps. His heart was pounding harder than ever, and he thought he was going to fall down and die.

He didn't. Slowly his breathing eased, his heart slowed, and his throat and lungs felt better. He wiped sweat off his forehead and struggled to stand. Once up, he felt better and turned to walk back to town. He was at least a mile down the South Road. Damn, how had he gotten way down here?

No houses, nothing out here. Slowly he remembered the area, yes, south of town. Johnson lived out this way, the guy with the wife with big tits. Huge tits. He'd always wanted to grab them and play with them when the woman came in the store. But she was the standoffish kind, and he was afraid to try anything.

He came to the Johnson house and paused. Lights were on

70

in the room at the side of the house. It could be her bedroom. He eased up to the house. Good, no dog. He slid along the side of the structure to the lighted window. The blind had been drawn, but not all the way down.

One lamp burned on the dresser. He looked at the bed not more than three feet from the window. A naked Sadie Johnson lay on top of her husband. They were screwing up a storm. She leaned up on her arms, and her big breasts rolled and swayed. She was riding the man below her as if he were a heifer and she were a range bull pounding it to him.

She rocked back and forth, built up a rhythm, and slammed forward. He could hear the man grunting. Mrs. Johnson drove at him again and again, then she gasped for breath, a scream bellowed from her mouth, and she trembled all over. Her hard thrusts stopped, and she dropped on top of him, shivering and shaking like an aspen leaf in a windstorm.

"Oh, God! Oh, God! Oh, God!" the woman screeched. Then she lifted and began pounding at the man again. He grabbed her and rolled her over, flattening her huge tits. He evidently was still inside her. He lifted her knees and began jolting against her, pounding into her, with his hips hitting her harder and harder. The woman screeched again.

A dog barked.

The man in the long black coat ran from the window, back to the road. He felt his massive hard-on. It bulged like a Douglas fir log in his pants. He'd have to do something about that.

He walked faster, thinking about his wife. She never said no to him when he wanted her. He'd get on home.

Ten minutes later, he walked into town, where he came to the back of the livery barn. The screaming in his head came again. The voices kept yelling, "blood, blood, blood."

He eyed the livery for a moment, then walked toward the back pasture. Yes, a dozen horses there. Most stood near the rear fence, sleeping on their feet. He slipped up on them quiet as any Indian and watched them.

They moved a little, but mostly stood with heads down,

feet splayed out so they wouldn't fall down as they slept. He crawled between the barbed wire strands of the fence and walked up to the closest mount. A sorrel he figured. He talked softly to the beast, came up on her side, and when he was at her head, she lifted it and nuzzled him.

It was what he waited for. His six-inch knife slashed across the horse's throat once, then again, then six more times, He forced the blade upward, driving it deeply into the flesh. The last time his hand and arm came back covered with blood, and the horse was screaming in chorus with the voices in his head.

The other mounts in the pasture bolted away. The mare he stood beside started to run, but didn't have the strength left. She went down on her front feet to her knees, then screamed again and fell to one side.

He was through the barbed wire by that time, running away from the livery.

He ran almost home, then stopped at a neighbor's outdoor well and washed the blood off his hand and arm and some from his black coat.

He hadn't heard the voices since the mare screamed in her death agony.

By the time he got home, he'd been gone two hours. He sat on the side of the bed and pulled off his clothes. When he lay down, his wife woke up. She saw him and smiled and turned toward him. One of her hands crept down to his belly, then to his crotch, and caught at his genitals.

"Hey, I can help you go to sleep. Remember how we used to do it every night? We'd have a long, slow, quiet lovemaking and then afterward you could drop right off. Remember? Let's try it again, a long, slow, easy, quiet, wonderful poking."

He remembered Mrs. Johnson's big tits, swaying and bouncing. He came erect at once and reached for his wife's breasts. Not as big but plenty to hold on to. Yes, he thought, this might be the best way for him to get to sleep. At least for tonight.

• • •

The next morning, Jessie and Ki had breakfast at the hotel dining room. They had been too tired the night before to do any planning.

Ki had told Jessie about the names that Ruthie had given him during their night of sex. They both had pushed the names into the background while they made another all-out effort to find the two other gold prospectors up the river.

Now Jessie frowned and pointed her fork at Ki. "A couple of days ago you said that Chad Bannington had been in town. Ruthie said that he could have been here when both our mill men were murdered?"

"That's what Ruthie said. Bannington is capable of doing this and much worse. It just depends on what he's getting out of it, and on this one, I don't see how he can profit by these two torture killings."

"If he's really still in the general area, and he killed the men, he had some kind of an angle on it. He did it for somebody or to spite somebody. Just to kill two men who worked for me wouldn't be enough. No cash money for him in that."

They talked about the half dozen times they had tried to get Bannington, when he was involved in one escapade or another. Each time they found him, they had ruined his project or his scam and blasted him out of town. But each time he escaped in the confusion. Now maybe they had a chance to nail him.

They finished their breakfast and sipped at second cups of coffee.

"Who were the other two names?"

"A phoney called Count Andre Malenkov, who Ruthie described as a tall, good-looking con man and gambler who seems to have plenty of money without doing much to get it. She said he's an inch over six feet tall, from Chicago not Russia, thin as a scarecrow, and an excellent dresser with gray hair and glasses. She figured Malenkov was about forty years old."

"I can ask Sheriff Kellerman about him."

"Oh, one more thing. Ruthie said to check with the sheriff to see if either of the bodies had been sexually violated. She says she swears that this Count Malenkov is queer."

"Probably too late to check that now. We'll see. Who's the third name you squandered your money on?"

"Ruthie says his name is Lunt Rockford. He has something of a reputation as a rounder and outlaw, but he's never been in trouble in Idaho that she knows of. He doesn't live in town but shows up once in a while and patronizes Ruthie when he comes. She figures he might be on a mine or a claim somewhere. Says he comes in town once every two months or so. Evidently he slips in, because most of the men here hate his guts. They rode him out of town on a rail about ten years ago, and don't like to see him back here."

"So she gave you a con-man queer, a sometimes outlaw who got thrown out of town, and our old nemesis Chad Bannington. One lives in town and two don't. It's going to be tough to check up on the two outlanders. First we'd have to find them."

"Which leaves us Count Andre Malenkov to look over first," Ki said.

They paid their bill and wandered outside. From the hotel's front steps, they could see the mighty Salmon River racing past the town.

"Somehow the river's got to be involved in this whole thing," Jessie said. "I've just got a feeling."

"Why don't I try to check out the count. Maybe he's in a poker game at one of the two gaming houses in town."

"Remember you're not the world's best poker player," Jessie said, grinning.

Ki frowned. "I do have some trouble with the curious all-Western mind. These men play poker with a combination of hunches and pure emotion. Poker should be played as an exercise in logic, memorizing the cards played and calculating the odds."

"Don't lose more than twenty dollars to him," Jessie said. "I'm going to talk to the people at the general store. It seems that if this Rockford character has a place around here somewhere and comes into town every two months, he must have to buy some provisions. Where better than the general store while he's here unloading his troubles to Ruthie?"

Ten minutes later, Jessie stood at the counter in the general store. No other customers were there. The woman co-owner's name was Nona, and now she rubbed her chin as if trying to remember.

"Lunt Rockford? I do recall a Rockford who lived here maybe a dozen years ago. Don't recollect if his name was Lunt."

"From what I hear he comes in town once every two months or so for supplies. I'd guess quite a sizeable order. You'd remember that I'm sure. He evidently got into some trouble here in town about ten years ago and got run out of the place."

"Oh, goodness, I don't remember that. I try to think only kind thoughts about people." She frowned, her hands busy on the counter. "I will try to remember. My husband isn't feeling well today, but I'll ask him when he's better. He might know some of the people I don't. I usually leave the store about four in the afternoon, and he keeps it open until seven every night. As a service to the people of Ruggins."

"If you think of anything, I'm staying at the hotel."

Nona nodded, and Jessie turned and walked out of the store. She couldn't figure out if the woman was lying to her or if she was a little addled and actually couldn't remember.

Jessie went into the women's apparel shop and bought a silk scarf. As she paid for it, she asked the matronly owner of the store if she had heard of Lunt Rockford.

"Rockford? Well, I should say I know about him. Everyone who's been in town for seven or eight years knows about Lunt Rockford. He came near to getting hanged, he did. We found out he was having his way with the young girls in our town. Fourteen- and fifteen-year-olds.

"The men got together, stripped him, tarred and feathered him, and rode him out of town on a pole, then threw him in the river. It ain't too swift a current right here, so he got out

75

alive, but no love lost for no Lunt Rockford, not in Ruggins there ain't."

"Oh, well, thank you. I heard the name mentioned, and I just wondered."

Jessie tried to remember about the widows of the murdered men. Neither of them could have a girl the right age. The one had no children; the other's wife had an oldest of ten or twelve. Those violated girls would be twenty-four or twenty-five by now. That angle didn't hold up.

Still, Lunt Rockford could be a suspect for some other reason. If he came to town once every two months, the primary trip would be for supplies. Where else could he get them if not at the general store? Nobody else handled items he would need if he lived twelve to twenty miles north or south of Ruggins.

He could come after Nona Henshaw went home. Possible, but each time? Another possibility was that Nona knew Rockford perfectly well and didn't want to talk about it because of his bad reputation in town.

Jessie filed away the information and went to talk to the sheriff. The lawman was in and furiously attacking papers on his desk. He looked up at her and his scowl evaporated. He shook his head. "When I took this job, I didn't know about all the confounded legal paperwork involved. Sheriff sales, sheriff foreclosures, sheriff investigations, this and that and the other. Damn, don't leave me no time to try to solve my two murder cases—no, three cases." He stood and went over to meet her. He closed the door and bent and kissed her cheek.

"You missed the target," Jessie said. He kissed her again on her lips, and she clung to him a moment.

"That's more the kind of a hello that I like. You hear about our getting turned around at the ten-mile creek?"

"Did. Who could have killed your mule?"

"Indians, or white men. A bear wouldn't have a knife that sharp. Right now I don't know what to think. We found all kinds of evidence that the survey crew had been there, then we got turned back."

"I'll go along on the next trip, with a couple of deputies

and some firepower. I've developed a neat little device I call my hand bomb. Works like a charm and can cut down a half dozen men at a time, or Indians. I've never really used it against anybody. Usually just a demonstration of what it can do is enough."

"I'm willing to take all the help you can provide."

"Good. You hear about last night?"

"I slept like a drowned polecat."

"We had two animals killed, both with knives. Somebody slashed a dog into mincemeat, and somebody cut a horse's throat half a dozen times. The mount was in the livery's back lot."

"In this devil worship, isn't there something about blood rituals?" Jessie asked.

"I know almost nothing about that. If there is, this time the blood was not human; that's one consolation. On the other hand, this might have nothing to do with the two mill hand killings. This probably was two people: One hated the dog because it barked and kept him awake; the other one had a fight with the livery owner about charges or such. We're investigating both of those angles."

"Good. I've got three names for you to tell me about. First, Count Andre Malenkov."

"Met him. No wanteds on him. Cheats at poker now and then but never been flat-out caught bottom dealing or such. A man with no real visible means of support other than his gambling. Seems to have more money than he could make gambling here in town. No complaints, no arrests. Next?"

"Chad Bannington."

"Oh yes. That name I know well. I've got a dozen wanted posters on him. Hear that he's been in and out of town now and then, but I'm always too late or in the wrong place to nail him. His last bit of killing was over in Oregon. Robbed a bank, killed two employees, got away clean. Nobody knew about the robbery until the next morning, when the bank didn't open up.

"He went in just at closing time, pulled the blinds, knifed

77

the two who challenged him, tied up the third man in the bank, and cleaned out the safe and money drawers. Took every dollar in the place, even the loose change in the dead men's pockets. A real bad character. I want him."

"Good. We have a long-running fight with Mr. Bannington as well. We want him, too. I have him down as a suspect in the deaths of my two workers. What about Lunt Rockford?"

"Rockford? Rockford. Doesn't come to mind or remind me of any wanted posters. How long ago?"

"Ten years."

"Before my time. Let me call in one of my deputies. He's been here since the Garden of Eden."

A moment later, a deputy came in who wore a beard and more than fifty years of experience. The sheriff introduced him as Deputy Ira Livingston.

"Lunt Rockford? Sure. A scoundrel, no good. Got himself run out of town, tarred and feathered and thrown in the river."

"Has he been back to town since then, Ira?" Jessie asked.

"I hear he comes in now and then, but I never have seen him. No charges against him, but he's not a popular man in town."

"Ira, I understand he had a way with young girls around here," Jessie said.

"That he did, too much of a way. Three pregnant, three more left town just after he got thrown out."

The sheriff had been taking notes. "But no warrants or wanted posters on him?"

"No, Sheriff. That was before we had much real law here. Sort of took care of things ourselves. Half the town wanted to hang him. The other half won."

Sheriff Kellerman looked at Jessie. "Anything else?"

"How often do you figure he comes to town?" Jessie asked.

Deputy Livingston rubbed his face with one hand, then combed his fingers back through graying hair. "On average I'd say he's in town once every two or three months. We got no paper on him. I see him here and there. He don't advertise he's here. Funny, he never had any money when he lived here.

Now he seems to buy what he needs and leaves."

"He comes with pack mules?" Jessie asked.

"Fact he does. Think he'd have a wagon or buckboard or such, but he sticks to pack mules. Usually two of them."

Jessie thanked the deputy. The sheriff nodded at him, and he left the room.

"Enough?"

"Plenty. I just don't know what to do with it. There could be two potential suspects here for the town killings. Both men have been in town, could have been here when the killings took place."

"Not evidence I'd want to take to court," Sheriff Mark Kellerman said.

"Me either. Still it makes me do some thinking." Jessie changed gears. "The river. When do you want to go up the river and get that problem all sorted out?"

Chapter 8

While Jessie went to talk to the sheriff, Ki looked in the town's two gambling parlors for Count Malenkov. No one matching the count's description was in the first saloon. In the second one, he found the fake Russian playing in a four-handed poker game.

Ki watched from across the table as the hand finished. Malenkov looked up at him.

"You want in the game? You bring fresh money to the table, *nyet?*"

"I'm not much of a poker player," Ki said.

The phoney Russian grinned wider. "Good, good. Just the kind of man we want in the game. It's a quarter-limit bet. How much can you lose?"

Ki shrugged, bought in, and played two hands. The count was about as he had been described. Ki figured him at forty-three or forty-four. He didn't look six feet tall, but he might be. He wore a soft gray suit, with a gray vest and a watch fob with gold chain. His eyeglasses were the half-frame type that set well down on his nose, and he used them only for reading. The man's face was thin, more like a skeleton than a human form.

Ki lost a dollar and a half. The other three men dropped out of the game, and Ki called for fresh mugs of beer for the Russian and himself. Ki held the cards but didn't deal.

"Understand you know this town pretty well," Ki said.

"Well enough. I get by. You be that Japanese man in town looking for the killer of those two mill hands. Any luck so far?"

"Not that I'd write home to mother about. I was about to ask you to help me in that very matter."

"Oh," Malenkov said. His brows went up, and he adjusted his tie, then smoothed out his five-button vest. "Just how in the world could I help?"

"You said you know the town. I don't. Who would stand to gain by the death of those two mill hands?"

Malenkov sat back in his chair, laced his fingers together behind his head, and frowned. "I've wondered about that myself. From what I hear the bodies had the same marks on them, as if they were done by the same person.

"I don't know about the devil worship angle that some people are talking about. I don't much believe in that sort of thing. But the economic factor, that one I can't figure. Both men worked at the same mill, but they didn't move in the same circles, hardly knew one another. The wives totally different. I can't see how there could be any economic link at all in the two deaths."

"What about somebody who hated the mill or the manager and wanted to get back at it?"

"Could be a factor, but not a satisfying one for the killer. No, I'd think the motive for the killings lies elsewhere."

"That's what stumps me," Ki said. "To find a killer, I like to have a motive and opportunity, then I have a better chance of finding the villain."

Malenkov slicked back his gray hair with one hand, then took off his spectacles and cleaned them with a white linen handkerchief.

"That is a problem. I like to fancy myself something of a detective, but I find no clues at all to these ghastly murders. Nothing to point in any direction. At last I have concluded that the victims were chosen purely by chance."

"Chance? Just whoever happened to be passing by the killer when one of his killing moods struck?"

81

"That's my best logical conclusion on the matter." Count Malenkov lifted his brows. His thin face seemed to grow longer. "I'm sorry. I know that isn't much help. It's absolutely the worst kind of crime to solve. Nothing to build on, no logic to use to track down the killer, or to help avoid another death."

The fake count stood. "Well, sir. It's been interesting talking with you. I hope you find your man, or woman as the case may be. Now it's time for my morning constitutional. I try to get in a brisk two-mile walk every morning. Keeps the blood pure, fights off attacks of the vapors, and indeed, simply makes me feel better. I'm on my way. I'm taking the north road this morning."

The well-dressed man gave a short bow, clicked his leather heels together at the same time, and walked across the saloon and out the front door.

Ki finished his beer and stared after the man. Harmless— a fop and a fool, but not by any means a killer. Ruthie had probably put the man on her list because she didn't like him, and because he never used her services.

After the gambler went outside, Ki left as well. He leaned against the wall of the saloon and watched the town. A small, birdlike man crossed the street. He stood no more than five feet tall and was so thin his clothes hung on him as if they were about to slide off. He had a small, round face, almost no eyebrows, and thin lips.

He wore some kind of sandals on his feet and no stockings, and a pair of lumberjack's pants, with the bottoms cut off at mid calf so they wouldn't snag on brush or logs. His shirt had lost all but one button, and it wasn't fastened. The sleeves of the shirt hid his hands; only the ends of his fingers showed.

He stared at Ki for a moment then came forward, jumped from the dusty street onto the boardwalk, and pointed at Ki.

"You're that Japanese man in town looking for the killer, right?"

Ki nodded.

"Inscrutable, you Orientals are all inscrutable, and I can't tell what you're thinking. You found the killer yet?"

Ki shook his head.

"Not surprised. I was amazed when I found out. Oh, yes, I can tell you exactly who the killer is and why he did it. You see, I spend a lot of my time with nature and the birds, and I can see into the past and sometimes into the future. I'm psychic. That means I am highly sensitive to nonphysical or supernatural forces and influences." He watched Ki a moment, but the Oriental made no sign of understanding.

Then Ki laughed softly and stared back at the much shorter man. "Then I assume that you have extraordinary and mysterious sensitivity and understanding of all things, the way all of us mystics do."

The small man smiled. "You *do understand.* I'm pleased. Can you take me to Miss Starbuck? I'd like to set her on the right road to finding the killer."

"But you told me you know who the killer is."

"Of course I know. It's just that my mind's eye is not totally focused or centered, and I'm having a bit of trouble making it all come clear. But I have some highly interesting signposts and guidelines I'd like to speak with both of you about."

"What's your name?" Ki asked.

"I'm the Birdman of Ruggins. Or sometimes called the Ruggins's Birdman. Either one will do."

"I'm not sure just where Miss Starbuck is right now. Could we arrange to come see you this afternoon?"

The small man took a step back, his face showing shock and surprise.

"No, of course not. It has to be right now. I usually don't go this far to share my understanding with the people of Ruggins. I'm doing you both a great service by extending myself this much."

Ki grinned, doing all he could to keep from laughing. At last he nodded. "Let's go this way. She still may be at the sheriff's office."

Ki started walking, but the small man didn't move.

"I don't like the sheriff. He has great power, legal power,

83

and sometimes it conflicts with my own."

"If Jessie is there, I'll have her come outside to talk."

That satisfied the small man, and he walked along, a step in back as he tried vainly to keep up with Ki's long stride. Ki went inside the courthouse, to the sheriff's office. The Birdman remained on the sidewalk.

Ki found Jessie just leaving the sheriff's office. He noticed that her face was slightly flushed. He smiled, knowing the reason. Jessie didn't blush easily, but she did color up when she was kissed. She looked at him and her brows went up.

"I've found a little man who wants to talk to you. He says he knows who killed the mill hands."

"Knows?"

"He says he knows, but he can't quite make it come clear right now. Claims he's some kind of a mystic or psychic and wants to talk to us. He's outside, doesn't like the sheriff."

"I can't see why," Jessie said softly and Ki laughed. They went out to the sidewalk, where the small man waited.

"Jessie Starbuck, this is the Birdman of Ruggins. Birdman, meet Jessie Starbuck."

He bowed low, and when he came up, his hands were grasping each other. "I'm honored to meet the famous Jessie Starbuck. I'm sorry that a tragedy had to bring you to our community. Now, if you'll follow me, I'll take you to my home, and there I can tell you what I know about the two killings."

He set off without any approval by the two. Jessie shrugged, Ki lifted his brows, and they marched after the little man. He went off Main Street at the first chance, heading for the river. There, he followed the bank south for two hundred yards, then turned into a thick stand of quaking aspens. They came through the stand of aspens, and suddenly they were in a kind of open-air house.

It had a roof, conveniently made from slabs of sawn lumber that were irregular and edged with the bark which most lumber mills threw away or burned.

There were no walls. Uncut trees had been used as side

poles to hold up the roof. Many pines and spruce extended through the roof and soared high overhead.

At one side, a heavy growth of birch formed what amounted to a thick wall. Still the wind could filter through it. In most of the areas under the roof there were bird feeders. Dozens of birds flew in and out of the "house." Jessie saw a red, yellow, and black bird she remembered as a Western tanager. A pair of hummingbirds buzzed through an opening and were gone.

The Birdman pointed to a bench next to what could have been a wall. The bench was built between a Douglas fir tree and a spruce, both of which extended through the roof and fifty feet above.

"Oh, yes, you've not been here before. This is my home. I live here with the birds and now and then a deer and a few chipmunks and a friendly porcupine. We all get along fine."

"You feed the birds?" Ki asked.

"Yes. Not much need to in the summertime, plenty for them to eat, and I remind them about that. But habits are hard to break. When the snow is four feet deep outside, it's harder to find seeds and insects."

He sat on a stool made from an eighteen-inch section of a two-foot-thick log.

"Now, you said you know who the killer of my two mill hands is, Mr. Birdman. Would you tell me?"

The small man crossed his arms in a minor protest.

"I told your friend here that I know but I don't know. I've seen them in a vision, but I'm not certain if the man was the same both times. He wore different clothes. Once a long black coat. Once a short gray coat."

"Was the face the same?" Ki asked. "Did you see the man's face?"

"Of course!" The rejoinder came sharply. "I told you I have psychic powers."

"You recognized the man by his face?" Jessie asked.

The Birdman's eyes went wide, and his hands pawed the air in front of him. For a moment he kept his balance, then he stiffened and fell to the side off the stool. Ki caught him

85

before he hit the ground. There was no floor in the "house," only the forest ground cover.

Ki held the thin man for a moment, pushing him back on the log stool. The Birdman blinked, then gave a long groan and shook himself. He moved his head around in a circle as if testing his neck, then he shook just his head and his eyes opened.

"Yes, yes, I understand that you are anxious to know of the name of the man I saw killing the first man. You won't be happy with me, but I must be true to my calling. I must read the truth to any and all who will listen to it."

"Who killed the first mill worker, Birdman?" Jessie asked her tone stern, unyielding.

The Birdman looked at both of them, stood, and moved behind a small table that was set with all sorts of seeds and suet and some fresh fruit for the birds.

"The man who killed the first mill worker had the opportunity, had the power, and has the cover of his office. The killer was Sheriff Mark Kellerman."

Jessie's face flared with anger. She stood and turned away from the Birdman. "Ki, let's get out of here."

Ki had come to his feet when she did. Now he moved between her and the small man with the birdlike face and edged her to one of the many openings in the "house" wall. They were outside when Jessie turned.

"You pathetic little man. You must have an extremely low opinion of yourself to live this way and to claim to have powers which you don't have at all. Mark Kellerman could no more have killed those two men than you could. And heaven knows a poor excuse for a man like you could never find the courage or the anger to kill a man, let alone two of them. You spread that silly story to anyone else, and you're liable to find yourself riding a pole wearing a fresh coat of tar and feathers and taking a long swim down the Salmon River."

Ki caught her arm and pulled her up the trail toward town. He had only to urge her gently. At once Jessie closed her eyes, not quite sure of all that she had said to the hateful

86

little man but remembering enough to cause her to shake her head.

"Oh, the nerve of that little . . . weasel! How could he accuse Mark of killing those men? He's just a little fraud trying to impress people. I wonder how he lives. How does he buy his food? How does he stay warm in the winter? I'll ask Mark some questions about this little Birdman of Ruggins."

Ki chuckled softly. "It's a good thing I was between you and the little soothsayer. You glared at him like he'd just rustled ten thousand head of prime steers ready to be driven to market. You would have had him hung in five minutes if I hadn't been there."

Jessie lifted her brows and looked at Ki.

"That bad, huh?"

"That bad. You must think quite a bit of this lawman."

"He's a gentleman, a wonderful man, and I respect him as a lawman and as a human being."

Ki settled the braided leather headband on his head and grinned. "Yep, Jessie. You've got quite a thing going with this here Idaho Territorial lawman."

"Hey, samurai, we came here to do a job. That's the important thing confronting us. Let's get the work done." Jessie's face was a bit grim as they walked back to town.

Ki was pleased to see it ease a little as they entered the outskirts, and then, by the time they were at the hotel, she had settled her anger and was back in complete control.

"Lunch?" Ki asked. He had picked up the word when they were in San Francisco, where everyone called dinner "lunch," and where supper had become "dinner."

Jessie nodded, and they ate at one of the two cafes in the small town. They had ground venison on a bun, and Jessie was delighted with the taste.

"I've never had venison cooked that way before," she said. "It's interesting." For dessert they had mouth-watering red huckleberry pie.

"The red huckleberries are wild, grow in many of the mountains of the West," Ki said. "These are not like the blue huckleberries they grow in the East, where they call them blueberries."

Jessie looked at him in surprise.

"If it's good to eat, I like to find out about it," Ki said.

Over lunch, Jessie told Ki what she had found out from the sheriff and the general store woman about Lunt Rockford.

"He could be a player in this little drama," Jessie said. "I'm just not sure where he fits in. The woman lied to me about him. What I'm wondering is why. We should go see Brock Henshaw after his wife goes home. We can indicate that she told us that Rockford had been coming into the store regularly, and work it from there. Why the mules rather than a wagon? We might find out something interesting."

She filled him in on Chad Bannington, how he had been in town and the sheriff knew about him but hadn't been able to catch him yet.

Ki told Jessie about Count Andre Malenkov and how he was convinced that the man didn't have a hand in the two mill worker killings.

"We have too many loose ends on this one," Jessie said. "We have three crimes and no actual suspects. That worries me. We should have more than that by this time."

Ki smiled at her. "Jessie, what you need is another long, hot bath. After we finish lunch, you can go back to the hotel and have that long, hot bath, then a short nap, and we'll go see Mr. Henshaw at his store about four-thirty. That leaves me time for a good two-hour run out the north road. I want to look over the country up that way. I need the run for a bit of cleansing. That psychic was a little too much for even a mystic like me to swallow."

Jessie finished the huckleberry pie and nodded. "I agree with you about the bath. That sounds really fine. Just don't get lost in these great north woods. You could wander around out there for years and nobody would ever find you."

They met in the hotel lobby at four-fifteen as planned and walked down the block to the Ruggins General Store. Jessie waited until a customer left with her purchase, then approached the merchant who stood behind the counter.

"Mr. Henshaw, you know who we are. We have a few questions for you. Oh, is Mrs. Henshaw here?"

"No, she went home a few minutes ago."

"Then we'll just ask you. Earlier today, your wife told us that Lunt Rockford was a regular customer, that he came in every two months for provisions and supplies. She said he used pack mules for his return trip. That puzzles us. Why would he use pack mules to move north or south up the roads? Wouldn't a wagon be much more practical?"

Henshaw stared at her. "She told you about Rockford? I find that hard to . . . I mean by the saints in heaven, she wasn't supposed to tell you that." He wiped his hands on his pants and shook his head. "Nothing wrong with it; only Rockford doesn't have a good name in this town. Got thrown out ten years ago. So he comes late at night and we outfit him and get him on his way."

"But why the mules?"

"He likes them."

"He's a prospector then. I know lots of prospectors use mules back in the hills up north a ways."

"No, he isn't a prospector."

"Then, Mr. Henshaw, why would anyone use mules on a good wagon road?"

"He doesn't use the wagon road."

"Oh. Well, then I guess cross-country would fit in better. You know we used our mules to go back up the Salmon River. Does Lunt Rockford go up the same faint trail we found along the Salmon?"

Henshaw got busy with things on the counter. He took some items out of a shipping box and marked prices on them with a wax pencil.

"Mr. Henshaw. I asked you if Lunt Rockford took his pack mules up the Salmon River."

"I've never seen him heading up the river."

"But you know where he goes. Why don't you tell me? I

promise that you won't get in any trouble with him or with the city people. That's no concern of mine."

Henshaw took a long, deep breath. His hands trembled. At last he nodded. "Yes, he takes the mules up the river. He made me promise not to tell anybody."

"I won't breathe a word of it. Up the Salmon, the River of No Return. What does a white man do up there in the middle of Indian country?"

"I don't know."

He said it too quickly; he knew. All Jessie had to do was get it out of him.

"Mr. Henshaw. How many of my mill workers live in town here?"

"Fifty, sixty families, I'm not sure."

"Wouldn't you say that all of them buy food and clothes and provisions from you?"

"Yes, not much place else in town."

"Wouldn't you say that my mill management people order a lot of goods and materials and supplies through your store?"

Henshaw mopped his forehead with a white handkerchief. He stuffed it in his pocket and sat down on a high stool behind the counter.

"Yes, Mrs. Starbuck. Your mill people do a lot of business with me for supplies."

"How much more than Lunt Rockford buys?"

"A lot."

"Maybe two hundred times as much?"

"I reckon."

"What would happen to your store, Mr. Henshaw, if Starbuck Enterprises were to open a company store here? We could sell our goods at wholesale prices, cut below your prices by thirty percent. We could instruct our people to buy at our company store. How long do you think your store could last?"

"Oh, God! Maybe six months, and I'd be losing money every day."

"I don't want to do anything like that, Mr. Henshaw. What I want you to do is tell me why Lunt Rockford takes in supplies.

Who else is up that river? What are they doing up there? Do you think Rockford, or anyone else up there, might have had some part in the death of Page Dabrowski?" She paused. "Let's get started right now, Mr. Henshaw. I can see that you have a lot to tell me."

★

Chapter 9

Brock Henshaw stared at the woman in his general merchandise store in Ruggins, Idaho Territory.

"Usually, Mr. Henshaw, I don't have to threaten people," Jessie Starbuck said. "In your case it's justified. You have information I desperately need, and I'll do whatever it takes to get it. The lives of two of my workers may be in jeopardy. I want to rescue them. Now start talking."

Brock sat on the tall stool behind the store counter. He wiped his hand hard across his face, distorting his features. Then he let out a long sigh and shook his head.

"The pain to come. I dread it. As our great poet William Wordsworth said in his 'Character of the Happy Warrior': 'Who doomed to go in the company with pain, and fear and bloodshed, miserable train!' " He paused. "I promised Lunt Rockford I'd never tell a thing about his trips here, but looks like I got to. Yeah, he comes down for supplies. Depends on the time of the year. He has a couple of log houses upstream. I don't know exactly how far, he never told me that.

"The trail up the Salmon River out there is the only way in or out of his place. It's in the middle of the wilderness. Lunt says he went up there when he got thrown out of town here, to recuperate and to put together a dream he'd had.

"He wanted a place where men on the run could settle down

for a while and have absolute security. So they wouldn't have to worry about some sheriff or marshal or damn bounty hunter come charging through the door."

"These men you're talking about are outlaws, right?" Ki asked. "All wanted by the law."

"Yeah, that's what he planned for. He built himself a lean-to, then a small log cabin, and finally a larger one. He hooked up with some of the wandering Northern Paiutes and lived with them awhile, took himself a woman, and talked the Indians into helping him build a big log house.

"That was three, four years ago. His woman died of the pox that he brought back from somewhere. The tribe moved on to another part of the mountains, and Lunt came out to Ruggins at night to get supplies and to visit Ruthie.

"He put out the word about his hideout with letters, and soon men began to slip into town at night and talk to me here at the store. I'd tell them how to get up the river and sell them enough food for two days to make the trip. The next morning early the men would be on their way up the faint trail along the Salmon River."

"Enough of the history lesson. How many outlaws does he have up there right now?" Jessie asked.

"I don't know. Earlier on he had twelve, but I've seen some strangers come through town who must have been leaving there. They buy a horse and ride off downriver. Not so many been going up there lately. My guess would be about eight or ten men up there now, from the supplies he's buying.

"Oh, he buys whatever he needs. He charges these outlaws according to what they can pay. Some two dollars a day, some five a day for total security. They pay up gladly. For a while he had an old sawbones on the run living up there who patched up gunshot wounds and such, but the doc left a year ago for a better scam somewhere else.

"Eight or ten outlaws up there," Henshaw went on. "So one of them could have shot Page Dabrowski when he got in the wrong place. Lunt never has had any strangers coming upriver to his place. Them prospectors must have got too

93

close and Lunt saw them and put Dabrowski in the river full of lead."

"What else do you know about this place?" Ki asked. "Anything about guards? Any better route to get in there? Anything about who might be there?"

"Only big name I know who's still there is Chad Bannington. You heard of him?"

Jessie snorted. "Heard of him. Ki and I have been chasing him on and off for five years. You know for sure he's up there?"

"Yes. Lunt likes to brag a little. Tells me the top bad guys he has up there. Calls the place the Rooster's Nest. Says he's the top cock in the place and he calls the shots. If somebody doesn't like it, he's invited to take a rowboat down the river."

"That would be a death sentence."

"What they figure, too, so they calm down or hike out the next day."

"What about guards? They post any?" Jessie asked.

Henshaw laughed and shook his head. "Nope, no need. Figure no one is coming up there, because nobody knows the Rooster's Nest is there."

"How far is it up there?" Ki asked. "We've been upstream for at least ten miles. It isn't between here and there?"

"Lunt's never said. Must be over ten miles. He said something about a mule not being good for more than ten miles a day. He hated wasting two days each way."

"Which must mean about twenty miles to the Rooster's Nest," Jessie said. "Have you heard anything about them mining gold up there?"

"Never asked for any mining gear, not even any pans. If there's gold up there, they haven't found any. It's strictly a haven for the outlaws."

"They get all of their food from you?"

"No. Lunt says he's out hunting once a week for venison, elk, a moose now and then. They eat on the carcass as long as it stays fresh. He strips some and makes jerky of it. Then

94

he fishes a lot. During the summer he says he feeds the guys fish twice a week, and wild meat five times. Lots of berries up there, too. He buys mostly staples. Two years ago he took in a dozen baby chicks. So by now he must have three or four dozen chickens and laying hens and fryers."

"A regular gourmet's delight," Jessie said. "Now, what do I tell the sheriff about you? Withholding information about a known felon and a wanted man is illegal."

"Swear I didn't know that. Hey, I ain't the only one in town who knows about Lunt Rockford coming through here. He ain't even wanted."

"But Chad Bannington sure is," Ki said.

"You tricked me. You tell the sheriff I said any of this and I'll deny it. You don't have a disinterested witness. You couldn't prove what I said."

Jessie nodded. "I agree. No charges against you. We'll be taking a trip up the river tomorrow, I hope. Ki will be around to order some goods and to get another mule or two. You be ready. And don't overcharge me for the goods. I can still run you out of business anytime I want to."

Brock Henshaw nodded. "I might have known when I first saw you. As the writer William Morris said in his 'Love Is Enough': 'Love is enough; though the world be a waning, And the woods have no voice but the voice of complaining.' I know well how that bard thought about the complaining part."

"Enough of your poetry, Henshaw," Ki said. "If Lunt Rockford comes into town in the next few days, you *will come and tell Miss Starbuck at once*. Do I make myself perfectly clear?"

"Yes."

"Good. You don't have to mention our little conversation to anyone. Oh, you said that Rockford visited Ruthie when he came to town. Was this a regular thing with him?"

"Yes, it was part of his usual routine. He'd wait for darkness, then come to the store and put in his order. I'd get it ready and packed on his mule out the back door. Then he'd go to Ruthie's and spend the night. By four A.M. he'd pick up his mule at my home and be back upstream before daylight."

"Thanks, Henshaw," Jessie said. "You've done well. I promise this won't get you in any trouble. Just to set your mind at ease, I've decided not to open a store here, after all."

Jessie turned, and she and Ki walked out of the store. Once they were on the boardwalk, she turned to Ki.

"Time you paid another visit on Ruthie. No in-depth research this time. Just find out what she knows about Lunt Rockford, how far it is to his place, how many men are there, that sort of thing. Oh, you also might find out if she's ever gone into the Rooster's Nest to hear a little crowing from the customers up there."

Ki grinned. "A pleasure. It may take some time if she's busy."

"Time is what we're short of. After you wring all the information from her, go to the general store and lay in some supplies for our trip up river. Say for five days. I'd guess that the sheriff will furnish his own supplies for him and his men. I'm heading that way with this most recent news about his county he doesn't know about."

Ki grinned. "Try to keep it on a businesslike basis," Ki said and hurried away as she pretended to swat him.

It was nearly five-thirty by the time Jessie found the sheriff in his office. He smiled, closed the door, and kissed her lips gently. She eased away and sat in the chair in front of his desk.

"I have some news for you. Your county is harboring from six to a dozen wanted criminals."

Sheriff Mark Kellerman looked at her in surprise. "That is news. Just where are these misfits?"

Jessie told him the story, much as Brock Henshaw had told her. When it was over, the sheriff frowned at his desk, made some notes, and then looked up.

"Would tomorrow morning be too early to start a trip up the river?"

"Ki will get supplies for him and me from the store. I figured you might want to take some men with you."

Sheriff Kellerman stood and paced his office. "How many do I have I can spare? I only have six deputies. I'll call two in for double shift and have them stay here in town. That means I can take four with us. I better notify them right away."

The sheriff left the room and talked with his people in the big office outside. He came back in a few moments later.

"One man down sick, so we get to take only three with us tomorrow. Meet at the general store at six A.M. Then we can have an early start. We know where we're going this time; we can get there quicker. We'll bring supplies for me and my men and get a mule. Now, what else?"

The sheriff opened a drawer and took out a half stick of dynamite. He held it up. "One thing I found that comes in handy in almost any kind of a shootout with bandits and wanted men is a little extra firepower. I don't have a Gatling gun, or what I hear is called a machine gun, so I go this route. Watch."

He took up the stick of dynamite and then peeled six strips of medical adhesive tape off a roll. He stuck the ends of the strips on the side of his desk. From another drawer he took out a six-inch length of fuse.

With a sharp pencil point he made a hole in the end of the half stick of dynamite. He took from another drawer a slender silver tube slightly larger than the fuse. He pushed the fuse into the hollow end of the detonator tube, then pushed the solid end of the tube into the hole in the end of the half stick of dynamite.

"A small bomb," he said. "Light the fuse and it burns for about thirty seconds before exploding. Cut the fuse in half and it burns about fifteen seconds before going off. The explosion is fine, disrupts an enemy's concentration, might deafen him. If close enough, the concussion could damage him, but not fatally." The sheriff grinned. "I don't like to lose a battle, even a small one. So I give myself some extra insurance."

From his bottom drawer he took a sack that held inch-long, large-headed roofing nails. The heads were a half inch across.

He took one of these and fixed it on the stick of dynamite with some of the medical tape. Then he added two dozen more of the roofing nails to the six-inch dynamite stick, fastening them firmly against the dynamite with the sticky tape.

When he finished, he held up the device.

"What we have here is a hand bomb that can blast into shreds a room inside a building. It can also have a deadly effect on troops, or in this case a band of outlaws, if it hits anywhere within twenty yards of them. The roofing nails are propelled outward at tremendous speed, just like the fragments of an artillery shell that explodes on impact.

"One of these hand bombs landing in the middle of a group of ten men could easily kill or wound all ten of them. A handy little item I haven't been able to put to good use yet. You can bet that I'll have a dozen or so of them all taped up, fused, and ready to light and throw when we get to the Rooster's Nest.

"I'll experiment with fuses tonight outside town and see if I can find a fuse that will burn evenly so I can cut the delay time to ten seconds before the big bang."

Jessie shuddered thinking of the terrible wounds that such a bomb could inflict on the human body. "Just be sure that your friendly forces are far enough away and protected before you use those things," Jessie said.

Sheriff Kellerman nodded. "Don't worry. I don't make mistakes with deadly force." He pulled the fuse and the detonator cap out of the half stick of dynamite and put them in separate drawers of his desk. "What about Ki? Doesn't he use a gun?"

"Not when he can help it. He has other means of putting down an opponent. He throws the *shuriken,* the eight-pointed death star. He's a master with them and with any kind of a blade. Of course, Ki also has more than a dozen ways he can kill a man with his bare hands and his feet."

"So, I guess Ki doesn't need a six-gun or a rifle," Sheriff Kellerman said.

"Ki says the second day on the way in we shouldn't have a

fire. That's probably what gave us away last time to the guards of the Rooster's Nest."

"Cold meals for a day and no coffee," Sheriff Kellerman said. "That's going to be tough duty."

"You still want to leave here at six A.M.?" Jessie asked.

"Best time of the day to travel." He smiled and looked at her, from the top of her head right down to the pointed toes of her cowboy boots. "So what about tonight?"

Jessie flashed him a smile, kissed his cheek, and then stepped back. "Tonight I think we both better get some sleep. We're going to have five hard days on the trail."

Sheriff Kellerman scowled. "Oh, damn. Trouble is I agree with you. But we do have to eat supper. Would you be my guest?"

She said, "Of course," and they left for the cafe that Jessie hadn't tried yet.

When Ki left Jessie at the general store, he walked directly to Ruthie's place and knocked on the door, then went inside.

A man around thirty sat in a chair holding a magazine. He looked up, then quickly back at his reading matter. Ki stared at the man.

"Is she in?" Ki asked.

"Yep, busy."

Ki stood by the window, not wanting to sit down, not as at ease as he had thought he would be. Coming to see a whore on business was one thing, having to wait in line for her to get done humping the paying customers was another. He eased over to the door and started out.

Ruthie called to him from the hallway. "Hey, Japo, where the hell you think you're going?"

Ki turned and chuckled. "Looks like you're busy."

"Never too busy to talk to a friend." She came to the edge of the living room and waggled her finger at the man sitting there. "As for you, Long John, be with you in a few minutes. Think about me all naked and panting. From the looks of things, this is just regular business, not screwing business."

The one called Long John grinned and waved, and Ki could see the touch of a blush creeping out of his collar.

Ruthie caught Ki by one arm and dragged him down to the first room. It was a sewing room, with bolts of cloth, a newfangled treadle sewing machine, and lots of papers of pins.

"So, what's the progress on those names I gave you?" Ruthie asked.

She had closed the door, and Ki reached out and rubbed one of her huge breasts. She purred softly.

"Names. The Russian phoney count is a no-count. He couldn't kill a fly with a twenty-pound cannon ball. Not a suspect. Lunt Rockford is an interest. What I want to know from you is what you saw when Lunt took you up to the Rooster's Nest last year."

Ruthie's dark eyes widened, and her mouth dropped open. For just a moment her eyes crossed, and she shook her head.

"Now, who told you a silly story like that? Must have been Brock Henshaw."

Ki rubbed harder on her big breasts. "Ruthie, when Lunt comes in every month or so, he orders his supplies and lots of food, then comes over here for your special service."

Ruthie sighed and sat down in a reinforced chair.

"Hell, I guess you know. Yeah, he comes, and gets his money's worth. Once last year he said the guys wanted me to come up and they'd guarantee me five hundred dollars for two days of work at the Rooster's Nest. It took us two days to go up the trail and another two days to come back, but I cleared damn near six hundred dollars for the trip.

"Not that I'd go back again. Them cocks were so hard up the first time around was pure hell."

"So how many men were there then?"

"Twelve. Not so many now, Lunt tells me. He was in about three weeks ago. Not as many new men coming in. He closes up for winter. Too hard to pack in the supplies."

"Draw me a picture of the place. How far from the river? This side or the other? How are the log houses set? Are there any obvious defenses? Any lookouts you remember?"

Ruthie scowled at him, then went and found a pencil and paper and drew a map of the Nest layout. All on the same side of the river as the town. Two big log buildings, maybe twenty feet wide by forty feet long. They sat facing each other stretched along the side of the stream. Two other smaller log buildings, ones Lunt built himself.

"Indians?" Ki asked.

"Not for two or three years. They all went over to the Montana side of the mountains. Fewer white people over there and a hell of a lot more buffalo."

"Lookouts?"

"Hell no. No need for them. Nobody knows they're up there but Lunt and me. Or so they think. Time I was up there Lunt had some real hardcases. He told them up front that he'd kill any man who hurt me or made me cry. That straightened them up, but still they was a little rough from wanting it so bad."

"Anything else we need to know?" Ki asked.

"You and Jessie Starbuck and the sheriff are going up there tomorrow, ain't you?"

"Yep."

"Don't get your long john down there hurt. I want to see him when you get back."

"I don't intend to get shot full of holes."

Ruthie caught his left hand and pushed it inside the robe she wore so his hand touched her breast. "Why is it you never wear a gun?"

Ki's right hand moved to his belt, extracted a *shuriken*, and in one continuous move threw it across the room, where it stuck an inch deep into the door frame.

Ruthie's eyes went wide. "Oh, migod. I bet you can hit what you aim at."

"Usually within a quarter of an inch, unless I get hurried too much or someone grabs my arm."

"You . . ." Ruthie looked up. "You've killed men with those?"

"That's my job. If anyone threatens Miss Starbuck, they answer to me." He took out another six-pointed star and showed it to her. "It's called a *shuriken,* or throwing star. I can do most anything with one of them that a gunman can do with a six-gun, and I'm a lot less noisy."

"I like that long gun between your legs better. You got time for a quick one?"

"Later. Right now I have to get the supplies together for our trail into the Rooster's Nest." He rubbed her breasts and pinched her nipples.

"You take care of things here until I get back. Then we'll have a real session."

Ki hurried out of the room and through the front door. He had to get the supplies ready for tomorrow and then show Jessica the drawing Ruthie had made of the Rooster's Nest layout. There could be trouble taking the place if it had ten or twelve armed men inside. He'd just have to play it by ear.

★

Chapter 10

The trip up the river went easier this time. Ki and Jessie knew the trail by now, and the posse of six people and two mules covered nearly eight miles the first day. No problems. They had their last cooked meal that night, and Ki browned some cured ham in a skillet to make sandwiches for the next day.

The three deputies bedded down to one side, and Ki took a blocking position near the river. Jessie and Sheriff Kellerman sat talking in front of the fire.

"Tomorrow we may find more than we bargained for," Jessie said. "Eight to ten desperate men will turn ugly when we confront them."

"We'll be a bit ugly acting ourselves," Sheriff Kellerman said. "Especially if we can get close enough to throw our bombs. Each of my men has four. I have six, and I gave six to Ki. He also asked me to bring along some dynamite. We have thirty sticks in the pack. He can use the hand bombs as a detonator to set off any number of the dynamite sticks."

Jessie nodded. "We talked about it. If we can get close enough, he thinks we can put the fear of God into them with a nighttime blast on one of the big log buildings."

"Scare hell out of them, that's for sure." Kellerman hesitated. "I guess I don't need to warn you to keep your head down tomorrow when the shooting starts."

"Why? If I do that, I can't find a target to shoot at."

"You can use that peashooter?"

"You want to try to outdraw me?"

Kellerman laughed and shook his head. "Not in a hundred years. I'm no fast draw."

Jessie giggled. "Good. Neither am I. A fast draw never killed a man unless the one slapping leather first could shoot straight as well."

"Hey," the sheriff said softly. She turned, and his face was an inch away. He kissed her lips, came away, then kissed her again.

"Half the town is whispering that I'm sweet on you, Jessie Starbuck."

"Oh, is that half of the town right?"

"Couldn't be more correct." He leaned in and kissed her again. "I like the way you kiss. I like the way you hold me early in the morning when we're both tired." He grinned. "Of course I like all the loving in between as well."

"But not tonight."

"I know."

"Then don't get yourself all worked up."

"Woman, I get worked up just sitting beside you. Right now my old whanger is trying to bulge his way through my britches."

"I'll take your word for it." She picked up his hand and pressed it over one of her breasts. "I'm not exactly a cool cucumber sitting on a block of ice myself. Pet me just a little."

His hand caressed her breast a moment, then he kissed her softly on the lips and moved his hand away.

"This reminds me of those short fuses I cut yesterday on those hand bombs of mine."

She leaned in and kissed his cheek. "Then I better snuff out your fuse until a more convenient time. Good night, extremely wonderful man. We both better get some sleep."

Jessie went to sleep holding the sheriff's hand.

The next morning they were up and moving by daylight. The word had been given for no loud talk, no whistling or yelling.

Two hours later they came to the spot where their mule had been killed. It still lay beside the stream.

"I'll go ahead as a scout," Ki said. "We don't want to stumble into anything or anyone."

He moved ahead at a trot, and the rest of them continued at a slower walking pace. They noticed early in the morning that the trail was wider here, and they saw evidence of shod hooves from horses or mules.

"Looks like a lot more traffic up this way," Jessie told the sheriff.

He nodded. "Maybe several divergent trails come together here for the rest of the way up to the Nest," he said.

They continued, wading another feeder creek and prodding the mules along. Jessie was getting worried. It was going too smoothly. No problems so far. What was going to blow up on her first?

She marched along, watching the trail ahead, listening for any change in the animal sounds. They didn't seem to bother the birds as they passed nearby or under them.

She took a quick breath when she saw Ki ahead waiting for them. She ran to him.

"Smoke," he said. "Smell the wood smoke? We're downwind from somebody's fire upstream from here. Not sure what it is. I'd say it's not over a mile away. We'll work upstream a little more cautiously."

They moved another half mile, and the smell of the wood smoke in the virgin forest came sharp and acrid to their nostrils.

Ki held up his hand, and they all stopped in place. One of the mules rumbled a moment, then all was quiet.

A trumpeter swan shrilled out his call somewhere downstream. A pheasant frightened by a wandering lynx or cougar sailed past them twenty yards away and then had to beat its wings furiously to get across the wide expanse of the Salmon River.

Then all was quiet again.

A pair of mountain bluebirds sailed overhead and landed

on a low-growing syringa with white flowers on it.

The quiet closed in once more. Only the soft rustle of the aspen leaves and the chattering of the Salmon River over the rocks and boulders thirty yards away could be heard.

They all jumped as a rifle shot blasted into the stillness. It came from upstream, and Ki grinned.

"Hunter," he said. "Let me go forward as a scout again."

They waited where they were, and a half hour later, Ki came jogging down the path. He settled into the forest mulch between Jessie and the sheriff.

"We're making progress. The shot came from a lookout not more than a quarter of a mile ahead. He's watching the trail downstream. The interesting part is that to the right, up a creek on this side of the river, I saw at least five men working in a panning operation. They have two sluice boxes and even a rocker box. Looks like they're working the sand along the near side of the creek. Five men there and one in the tree with the rifle. He's in the crotch of a big birch tree, about ten feet off the ground."

"We can shoot him out," Sheriff Kellerman said.

Ki shook his head. "Too much noise. We'd have to fight all five of the others. I'll go around him, come up on the side, and hit him with a star. He won't know what happened."

Kellerman frowned.

"Sheriff, I don't have to prove myself," Ki said. "Wait here."

The sheriff was ready to protest when Jessie called his name softly and he shrugged.

"If he says he can do it, he will," Jessie said. The half-Japanese man vanished into the brush and trees beside the river and moved upstream.

Ki worked through the brush without making a sound. In his many years in the land of the white men, he had learned from the Indians how to slip through the brush and dry twigs and leaves like a silent shadow.

He estimated the distance upstream, then curved toward the sound of the water. He went far enough to see the target tree.

It was another twenty yards upstream. He adjusted and aimed for a large Douglas fir across from the birch.

Five minutes later he stood behind the fir. He had an open throw from there. The birch had a crotch about fifteen feet off the ground. A man sat there, legs swinging slowly. He watched downstream. Now and then he yawned and looked at a pocket watch.

He moved so his torso showed plainly. Ki worked his way closer. No reason to take a chance. When he was thirty feet from the tree, he stopped and lifted an eight-pointed *shuriken* from the special pocket in the top of his tough jeans. He cocked his right wrist and arm to the left, then threw, with his wrist giving a final flick of speed to the star.

It sailed straight and true, sliced into the side of the watcher's neck, and tore out through his throat. Blood gushed from ruptured carotid and jugular veins. The man's head fell forward, then his whole body seemed to curl, and he tumbled from the tree and crashed through a branch and a smaller tree before he smashed into the ground and didn't move. The rifle clattered down after the body, but the weapon didn't fire when it hit a bush and fell to the forest mulch.

Ki ran to the trail and upstream so he could see the placer miners working. Yes, five of them. Two had rifles near to hand. The others carried revolvers. He couldn't tell if any of them were guarding any others.

Keeping under cover, Ki ran quickly back to the rest of the attack party.

"Clear," he said. "We can move up and get a good look at the five men in the stream."

A few minutes later, they peered from behind a screen of brush at the stream fifty yards in front of them. The five men were working the sluice boxes and shoveling sand. No one person seemed to be in charge.

"I don't know if any of them are my prospectors or not," Jessie said.

"You never met them," Ki said. "I saw in the records that Page hired them later on."

107

"If my men were there and they saw Page die, they would surely be working under protest, which would mean there would be a guard. I see no guards."

"Then they must all be outlaws who Rockford has talked into trying their hands at gold panning," Sheriff Kellerman said. "We have four rifles. We could pick them all off before they knew where we were."

"No!" Jessie said, her eyes narrowed, a quiver of anger around her nose. "We won't simply slaughter them. Ki, get as close to them as you can without being seen. Then we'll put a round over their heads and tell them to surrender. If they want a fight, we can give it to them."

"When you fire, have all four riflemen stand out where they can be seen in a bit of a crossed fire," Ki said. "That will impress them. I saw two rifles standing near the five."

Ki ran through the woods, and worked down the side of the stream until he was thirty yards from the miners. When he stopped, Jessie nodded at the sheriff.

"All right, we step out, Sheriff, you fire one shot over their heads, and we'll see what happens."

They stepped into the open a little more than fifty yards from the miners, and Sheriff Kellerman put a round into the bank behind them.

Two of the men flattened out against the sand bank. One stood up straight and stared at them.

"You're out gunned, gents," the sheriff bellowed. "We've got rifles all around you. Lay down on your bellies, with your hands clasped behind your heads."

One man below fired a six-gun, but the range was too great. One man lifted up and ran for the edge of the brush. Ki stood and threw a *shuriken*. The eight-pointed star slanted through the air and cut deeply into the man's right leg, pitching him to the ground. He wailed and tried to stop the flow of blood.

Two of the men knelt, then went on their bellies in the grass near the far bank and laced their fingers behind their heads.

The other two, who had gone flat next to the bank, giving

them partial protection, began working upstream, away from the riflemen.

"Let's go get them," Kellerman barked. His three deputies and Jessie ran forward. Ki came out of his hiding spot and paced the crawlers along the bank but well out of the range of their pistols.

Sheriff Kellerman stopped, lifted his Springfield, and fired. The carbine spat out another .45-caliber round behind its 55 grains of black powder. The round hit one of the crawling outlaws in the shoulder and jolted him flat in the sand.

"You shot me, you bastards!" he roared. The next man lifted up and ran. All three deputies fired. Their rifles and carbines went off almost at the same time. Two of the rounds caught the running man and jolted him forward as if he'd been struck by a locomotive. He slammed into the side of the riverbank, sprawling in death, then gravity took over and he rolled down the bank into the shallow stream, his face and head vanishing underwater.

"Hold steady and nobody else has to die," the sheriff shouted.

Ki ran in and disarmed the wounded man, stuffing the six-gun in his waistband, then moving the man back near the two who had given up. The fifth man, wounded with the star in his leg, came in limping in front of a deputy. Jessie grabbed the two rifles and checked them. Both loaded.

"Who's in charge here?" Jessie demanded. The men looked up when they realized she was a woman.

Three of them shrugged; then the fourth, one of the unwounded, pointed to the dead man in the stream.

"Old Wild William over there was the head miner. He knew what he was doing. Rest of us were just learning and playing. Hell, nothing else to do up here."

"You men are all wanted outlaws," the sheriff said. "Right now I want your name and the state or territory you're from." He took out a notebook and a stub of a pencil and went to each of the men for the information. He got the name of the dead man from the others. None of them was Chad Bannington.

109

"How many more up at the Rooster's Nest?" Jessie asked.

One of the them scowled. "Hell, don't make no difference to us. Six of us down here and six more up there, including Lunt. He's not even on a wanted poster."

"Chad Bannington still there?" Ki asked.

"Hell yes. But he don't do no gold panning. Beneath him, he told us." The talker was one of the men who had given up. Ki produced lengths of leather thongs and tied the four men's hands behind their backs.

Jessie ripped the sleeves off one of the men's shirts and tied up the two wounds so the men wouldn't bleed to death.

Then she went to the talkative one.

"Now, what was your name?"

"Victor."

"You lost this time. You have a wanted poster on you?"

"Yes, ma'am. Nothing but a little stage robbery."

"I'll see what we can do about it if you help me. How far is it to the Rooster's Nest?"

"Three, maybe four miles. An easy trail."

"Only six men there, you said."

"Right."

"Do they have any guards out?"

"None. They don't expect visitors."

"Where are the two prospectors who found the gold here?"

"Not sure. Bannington had them last I knew. Talking to them. Arguing. He finally said if they didn't do what he told them, he'd cut off the right hand of each man."

"That sounds like Chad Bannington. But you don't know where they went after that?"

"No, ma'am."

"What kind of weapons do they have up at the Rooster's Nest?" Sheriff Kellerman asked.

"Every man who comes has a rifle and a pistol. Not much else. I mean no eight or ten rifles set away. Nothing like that."

Jessie and the sheriff talked. They decided to go up right after they had something to eat. They ate their ham sandwiches.

Ki boiled some coffee over one of the already burning fires. There was no problem about smoke now.

Jessie scowled for a moment. "Ki, would the sound of the rifle fire here be heard upstream for three miles?"

Ki shook his head. "Probably not, not with the wind blowing our way. I'd doubt it."

They moved the four prisoners into the shade, left one deputy to guard them, and warned him to be careful.

Ki took the point again as they moved upstream with their pack mules. They had traveled what Jessie figured was two miles when Ki met them.

"The Rooster's Nest is just around the next bend in the river," he said. "I saw part of it. Two log houses like Ruthie said. But there's a long open stretch this side of the buildings. No good way to slip up on them from the woods in back of them either. We'll need to do some careful planning."

As with the gold panning, they viewed the objective from a brushy spot just downstream. They were a little more than a hundred yards away and could see men now and then moving around the buildings and yard area.

"Not a chance to walk up there and surprise them," Sheriff Kellerman said.

"If we were above them, we could float down the river," Jessie said. "The water's calm and flat right here."

"The only way to get there is to make an approach through the woods at the end of the far house," Ki said. "Unless we wait until darkness and blow up one of the buildings with dynamite and scare the hell out of everyone.

"I can get to that far building working through the trees," Ki said. "I'll have to move slow. I've seen the Apaches move across an open chunk of sandy desert. They blend with the sand and move so slowly that you'll never see them unless you concentrate on the exact spot where they lay. I can move slowly from tree to brush to bush and make it."

"I'll get the dynamite," the sheriff said. He pulled back to where they had left the mules. Ki took off his shirt and adjusted a small cloth bag on his belt.

"I have six of the hand bombs," Ki said. "Also I have matches to light the fuses. If I get in trouble, I'll throw the hand bombs and retreat if I have to. That's the time the four of you here start putting rifle and pistol rounds into both buildings."

Jessie nodded. "Sounds good. What happens after you set off the charge under the building?"

"The dynamite will roust everyone out of the buildings. Then we can open our firefight and nail down as many as we can."

"Those buildings look solid as forts."

"That's how Rockford built them. I'm surprised he doesn't have firing slots. If they hole up inside, it'll be a long fight to drive them out."

The sheriff came back with the dynamite. He had twenty sticks in a burlap bag.

"All twenty sticks will make a whale of an explosion," Sheriff Kellerman said.

"Exactly what we want." Ki kept the six-gun in his waistband, hefted the burlap bag of dynamite over his shoulder, and gave a mock salute before he walked away through the trees.

They saw him once as he flitted from a huge Douglas fir into a stand of birch. He was still fifty yards from the end building.

After that, they settled down to wait. The sheriff moved his men into firing positions. They cleared a few branches from in front of them and worked out a prone position to make as small a target as possible.

"Keep well in the brush," Jessie told the men. "That way the white smoke from the black powder won't be seen from the houses. If you take any return fire, you have to shoot once, then roll to a new position."

Jessie looked at her Waterbury pocket watch. Ki had been gone for twenty minutes. So far no sign of trouble. He was in an area now where the brush concealed him from their view.

Jessie had built a firing spot close to the sheriff. She had picked up one of the rifles the gold panners had. It was a fairly new Spencer .52-caliber with a full seven-round tube in the stock. She had a pair of the dynamite hand bombs pushed into her hip pocket and matches in her jeans front pocket, but she had no plans to light them. They would be the weapon of last resort.

"How much daylight do we have left?" Jessie asked.

"Doesn't get dark until at least eight o'clock this time of year," Sheriff Kellerman said.

Just then the quiet of the pristine Idaho wilderness ripped into a thousand pieces and a ear-drumming thunderclap exploded through the woods. Ahead they could see a cloud of black smoke and pieces of wood sailing into the sky before they slowed, stopped, and fell back to earth.

The rumble of the explosion seemed to hang in the air as the smoke did. Then they heard it echoing down the river valley. Jessie put her hands over her ears, but she was too late. Her only thought was to wonder if Ki had been far enough away from the massive bomb when it went off.

★

Chapter 11

Ki dove flat on his stomach behind a big Douglas fir and folded his arms over his neck only seconds before the bomb went off under the large log building in the Rooster's Nest. He felt the swoosh of hot air blasting past him and saw the retina-burning flash of the explosion no more than fifty feet ahead of him. He was deafened by the massive sound.

Ki had planted all twenty sticks of dynamite under the corner of the log building. They should have used heavier logs for the first row. He found where animals had dug a small burrow under the log on the end. He scooped out more dirt, then lay the bomb in place and put the half stick of dynamite, with the detonator and fuse and the nails, below the rest of the explosives. He lit the fuse and ran as fast as he could before he dove behind the big fir. It had shielded him from the worst.

Much of the force of the big bomb jolted straight upward. It blew off a six-foot section of logs on both sides of the corner, and left the roof sagging and near collapse.

Ki looked around the Douglas fir and stared at the debris of what had been the corner of a fine log building. He spotted no one inside. Three men ran from the end door of the other big building.

"What in hell was that?" one of the men bellowed.

"Whole damn end of the building blew itself up," someone answered.

The other one turned and ran. "Sounds like lawman work to me," he shouted. "I'm getting the hell out of here."

A rifle round from the front cut his legs out from under him, and he hit the ground on his hands and shoulder and rolled once, then lay still, screaming in pain.

The sure, steady voice of Sheriff Mark Kellerman boomed into the area.

"You men are all under arrest. This is a sheriff's posse and we have you surrounded. Come out now, give yourselves up, and none of you will be killed."

As soon as he finished talking, two rifle shots blasted into the mountain stillness, shattering two windows on the big lodge that had not been dynamited. The two men in front of Ki by more than a hundred feet turned and ran directly toward him and away from the rifles.

Ki pulled the six-gun and blasted two shots at the men. The rounds fell far short, but the pair of outlaws stopped, evidently thinking they were surrounded. They dove to the ground, whispered a minute, then came up charging for the undamaged log building. They were too far away for effective use of Ki's throwing stars. The two dashed into the building and slammed the door. One man lay groaning in pain in the dirt out front of the log building. Where were the other three?

Ki ran through the light cover to the left, away from the two men and along the side of the second building, undamaged except for the windows on this side, which had been blasted into shards and jagged points by the explosion. Ki saw one man in the wreck of the first building. He held one hand over a bloody face, and he staggered toward the undamaged end of the building. The man count was up to four. Where were the other two?

Out in front, the sheriff's rifles fired, keeping up a steady pace of a round every ten seconds.

Twenty yards down from the fractured log house, Ki could see a third, smaller house that Rockford had built himself. The logs slanted upward on the near side and had not been notched evenly. The door stood open and over it a sign said, "Head

115

Cock's Roost." Could be Rockford's office or his quarters. Maybe his summer quarters, where he could get away from the others.

Ki ran through the brush, to the back of the small log house, then worked his way around it to a window. The foot-square panes of glass were dirty on the outside, but he could still see through.

Inside was a bed, a table, and a chair. In the chair sat a man with a shattered right arm. A second man knelt in front of him, working on the arm, trying to stop the bleeding. These two men brought the count to six. That was the last of them.

Ki moved on to the end of the wall. By stepping around the corner he would be seen by those in the undamaged end of the other log house. Ki decided it was a risk he had to take. He went around quickly to the door and darted inside just as the unwounded man drew his six-gun.

Ki took three quick steps and threw out a *mae-tobi-geri,* a forward flying kick, which struck the six-gun man in the chest and slammed him backward over a chair. He dropped the weapon, and Ki closed on him just as he stood. Ki lashed out with a *choku-zuki,* a short forward punch, with his fingers together and stiff to form a deadly knife-like weapon.

Ki's fingers jolted into the gunman's windpipe, then slanted off, dazing the man. His eyes went wide just as Ki's elbow strike, an *empi-uchi,* hit him on the forehead and knocked him down and into unconsciousness.

Ki checked the wounded man. He would cause no trouble. His shattered arm had taken all of the fight out of him. Ki finished wrapping the arm so it wouldn't cause the man to bleed to death, then tied his feet and the other man's hands and feet and looked outside.

He had been conscious of firing from the direction of the first log building. It was at least forty feet long, built straight and true as if a real log-house expert had done the job.

Ki peered out the door again. He saw rifles aimed out glassless windows. Their attention was in the other direction. He ran from the small log house to the end of the battered one, stepped inside, and as he had figured, there was no one there. The firing came from the other building. This one appeared to be a barracks, dining hall, and recreation room. There evidently had been a kitchen in the end that he dynamited. It was little more than useless rubble now.

Ki looked out the gaping hole in the building, at the one where the last two men must be holed up. He saw a doorway on the end. Several windows had been shot out on both sides. Rifle bullets going all the way through the open structure, perhaps.

He ran to the near end of the second building and paused. Just above him he heard the quick firing of a repeating rifle. He swung out and saw that the window above him had been broken.

Ki reached into his small bag and took out two of the dynamite bombs. He struck a match and lit the first bomb, held it for three seconds, then threw it through the window with enough force that it would land near the window on the other side.

Ten seconds later the explosion ripped through the building, and he heard the roofing-nail shrapnel peppering the inside. The remainder of the window above Ki blew out. Smoke gushed from the opening. That told Ki that there were not many partitions in the big structure, perhaps as in the first one.

From inside the window came a long scream of agony and fury. A voice bellowed some words that were strangled and that Ki couldn't understand.

That should be five of the men down or wounded and out of action, he thought.

Ki worked down the building to the third window from the end and waited. All was silent for a moment, except for some staggered fire from the rifles aimed at the big log structure. No bullet would go through the foot-thick logs of Douglas fir. The windows were another matter.

A moment later Ki heard firing from above. He threw another of the small hand bombs through the nearby window.

It went off with a startling roar, and Ki guessed that most of the energy and nails blasted out the window just over him. So here there were walls inside.

The windows were a foot square here as well, and were not convenient to crawl through. The doors on each end would be locked and barred by this time. He could do little more here. Time to get back with the main body out in front.

Ki sprinted into the woods twenty yards behind the big house and had just passed a half dozen big firs when a rifle round whizzed within a few feet of him. He stood behind a tree, and the gunner from the log house lost sight of him. Ki rested for two minutes, and when he darted to the next tree and into the heavy concealing brush, there was no more fire at him.

He found Jessie in front and a little closer to the buildings than where he had left the group. They had taken some return fire, but no one had been hit.

He told Jessie and the sheriff about his adventure. "So I'd say that three of them are down in the back area. You chopped one down out front. Is he still there?"

"He's squalling like a baby for a doctor," Jessie said. "Which means he might not be hurt too bad."

"So that leaves three of them in the first log building," Sheriff Kellerman said. "How do we get them out of there?"

"Neither of the two men in the small cabin was Chad Bannington," Ki said.

"With his kind of luck he's one of the two still in the big log house," Jessie said. "Who has an idea how we can get them out of there without a frontal assault?"

"I could slip around and get under their line of fire and toss the hand bombs through the windows," Ki said. "I used two of them in back, and they are terrifyingly effective."

"I want Bannington alive so we can see him hang," Jessie said.

"How about a demonstration?" Sheriff Kellerman asked. "We get close enough to lob the bomb at a target near the building and show them what the bombs can do. Then we give them five minutes to come out with their hands up or we throw the bombs through every window in the place."

"Yes, it should work," Jessie said. "How do we get close enough to give the demonstration?"

Jessie answered her own question. "I'll talk to them while Ki slips up under cover," Jessie said. "When he's ready, he signals and I tell them about the surprise."

Ki worked his way through the bush toward the log house. He got within forty yards of it and ran out of concealment. He pointed to a six-foot Douglas fir growing about halfway between the log house and him.

Jessie understood. Kellerman had his men stop firing.

"You men in the house," Jessie called. "We don't need to kill you. All you have to do is come out with no weapons and your hands up. To show you you're in a hopeless situation, we have a little demonstration for you. See that six-foot fir in front of your house. Watch what our new hand bombs do to it."

Ki lit the fuse on the first bomb and threw it. It landed five feet from the tree, and when it went off, a dozen branches sagged and fell where the deadly roofing nails had cut them off.

Ki threw another bomb, and this one hit almost under the perfectly formed tree, and when the smoke cleared away, the tree stood with only a few bedraggled branches.

"Our little bombs can cut up a body much more than that," Jessie called. "Now, all you have to do is walk out with your hands clasped behind your heads."

They waited for five minutes. Nothing happened. Nobody moved. Ki scurried back to the better protection of the brush and trees.

"What's going on?" he asked.

Jessie shook her pretty head. "Nothing. They're up to something. We just don't know what."

Ki scanned the area again. The Salmon River came within fifty feet of the far end of the log cabins. He thought he saw something move. There, again!

"Somebody moving down by the river," Ki said. Then they

all saw him. A man pushed a small boat into the river. The slow water along the shore floated it, and the man jumped in with two oars. Ki darted across the open spot, zigzagging so a rifleman would have a hard time hitting him.

No rounds came. He made it to the beach and saw another boat, eight feet long, resting in the shallow waters. It had oars as well. He pushed the boat into the water and rowed into the current. He could see the man ahead of him just going out of the placid water and entering a series of small rapids.

The boat ahead slammed into the white water, tipped high, then righted itself. The man in the boat lay low, holding on with both hands as his little craft was jolted and smashed by the white water and scraped over rocks just under the surface.

Two minutes later the boat was through the white water, and the man rowed on downstream in a flat section of the Salmon.

Ki came to the white water quickly. He shipped his oars, and held on to them and the sides of the rowboat. He braced his feet under the seat and held tight as he entered the rapids. They looked calm and easy compared to some he had seen downstream.

The first jolt almost tipped the boat upside down. The bow rose high in the air, and the tail end was caught in a current that spun it around so it hit more white water sideways. One of the oars slipped from Ki's grasp and floated away. He kept hold of the second one as the boat bounced and grated over rocks, spun in a current, and then was battered with a wall of white water he thought would swamp it for sure.

Water splashed over him like a unending wave, and he had to gasp to get his breath. The boat was half-filled with the river water, and Ki felt his hand getting numb where he held the last oar.

Then the boat slipped out of the white water into the calm. Ki grabbed the oar and used it as a paddle, pulling hard on one side and then turning the blade in the water to act as a rudder and steer him where he wanted to go.

That's when he heard the roar. Ahead the Salmon River

simply vanished. It went to a certain point, and then he couldn't see it. The rapids ahead were five times as bad as those he had just came through. He saw the other man's boat in the middle of the river and the outlaw paddling for the brink.

Ki shook his head and stroked through the current for the shore. He was thirty feet away and knew he couldn't get the boat through the strong current to the sandspit he had aimed at. He made one last try, then stood and dove into the water, swimming with a strong overhand stroke and kicking his feet like a pair of steam-engine propellers.

He fought the current, felt himself swept downstream, then gave one final try, kicking harder, stroking with every ounce of energy in his body. He kept his head under water for two strokes, then came up for breath and felt his hand strike the bottom as he pulled. Gladly he dropped his feet to the bottom of the shallow water near shore and stood.

He saw the other boat near the lip of the ten-foot falls and rapids. Ki's empty boat would be there soon. Ki scrambled to shore and rushed down the bank, to where he could see the dropoff and the rocks and boulders below it in a hundred-foot-long rampage of white water.

The outlaw's boat tipped over the brink of the dropoff and slanted sideways. The human form inside held on, braced somehow until the boat hit the water again, then it crashed into a huge boulder and the boat righted itself, the man still inside.

The swift current caught the boat sideways and smashed it against another rock, then a third before it came out of the first battering. The man was still inside.

The next dropoff was higher than the first, and the boat left the top and turned straight down, bow-first, and twenty feet below hit a boulder with crashing force. The wooden boat shattered into a hundred pieces, and the man inside splashed into the white water with the debris.

For a moment, Ki couldn't find the man. Then he surfaced, struggling, his arms flailing the churning water. He tried to move toward shore, but another swift current caught him and threw him over another small drop of only three feet, but below were jagged rocks shattered by some long forgotten upthrust, or perhaps broken off by the ice that had frozen in the cracks of its broad expanse during winter and eventually cracked off huge slabs.

The man hit the jagged rocks and hung there a moment, then fresh currents of the greenish white water caught him and swept him off the rocks and downstream.

Ki saw him floating facedown in the water. Then his head struck a large rock and he was pulled under again. For five minutes Ki watched, but he could find no trace of the man. No human being could live through that kind of punishment. He must be dead, whoever he was.

Ki turned and trudged back up the trail toward the Rooster's Nest. They might never know who the man was who had foolishly tried to ride down the River of No Return.

Back at the log cabins, all was quiet. A deputy met Ki and told him they were in control, and all but one man was accounted for.

"Must be Chad Bannington," Ki said.

"Sheriff Kellerman talked to the prisoners in the small cabin," the deputy said. "They told him that Bannington always said he could ride down the river if the law ever got up here. Said he knew how, he'd done it before.

"Bannington and Lunt Rockford holed up in the fort, as they called it, as soon as the shooting started. Lunt told the men that he had an escape plan, too. Said he'd scamper out the back door with his mule and be over a Paiute trail five miles before anyone knew he was gone."

At the main log structure, Ki told them what had happened to the man they decided must have been Bannington. "No man could live through what he suffered going down those second falls. He was broken and smashed into pulp before he was halfway down. He might surface downstream when the body gets all swollen in three or four days."

Jessie sobered. "We've hunted him for a long time. He told us we'd never take him alive. I guess he had the last word on that."

Jessie had patched up the other wounded man. They got the name of the dead man who had been on guard duty in the tree down at the placer mine. Jessie herded the four survivors together at the Nest and eyed them sternly.

"You men know that the two prospectors were captured up here. We haven't found them. Who knows where they were taken?"

The unwounded man looked at Jessie.

"I know. Bannington told them they had to find the mother lode of that placer gold. He took them up that same creek. He took another man with him to guard the prospectors. Told the guard he'd get fifty percent of whatever they found. Then Bannington came back and left the guard with them."

"Up the same creek the placer is on?" Kellerman asked.

The man nodded.

Jessie made up her mind in a trice. "Let's saddle up here and get moving back downstream. We'll get to the placer mining setup and stay overnight there and hope we can find the other two prospectors before dark tomorrow."

It was less than three miles to the placer creek. One of the prisoners there confirmed the name of the dead man from the lookout tree. Sheriff Kellerman noted it down, along with the other wanted men in the company.

The deputy sheriff who had stayed to guard the placer creek prisoners said nobody had come by him all day. Sheriff Kellerman picked two men to go with him and Jessie up the creek to hunt for the prospectors. Ki would keep control of the prisoners at the placer site.

Jessie frowned a moment, breaking up her pretty face. "Now all we have to do is find the two prospectors. They should be able to tell us for sure who killed Page Dabrowski." She waved at Sheriff Kellerman and his two deputies. "Let's get this show on the road, Sheriff. I want to find my two men and be sure they're safe."

★

Chapter 12

Jessie insisted on taking the lead working their way up the small stream. It was twenty feet wide in places but never more than a foot-and-a-half deep. The water had carved out a small valley, and soon the sides of the hills closed in the on them and they were in a canyon, with the stream in the bottom and the land lifting up on each side.

They came to a particularly sparse wooded area, and Jessie stopped with them still under the cover of the Douglas fir and Western hemlock. She scanned the side of the canyon.

"More than likely any mother lode would be up the side of the hillside somewhere. Watch for upthrusts of rocks that look like they've been pushed upward by some earth-shattering force. Often these upthrusts will bring gold ore with them if it's about."

They scanned all of the hills on both sides but couldn't even find any outcroppings.

They crossed the open area and waded back into the shade of the old-growth forest. With all the rain, there was a good supply of undergrowth. The team stayed near the water to outwit the tangled brush and fallen trees as best they could.

Jessie guessed they had come a mile. The creek seemed as wide and chattering as ever. She wondered if the outlaw who had told them the prospectors had come up here looking for the mother lode had lied to them.

A hundred yards later, Jessie's nose twitched and she smelled the acrid tang of wood smoke in the air. She paused, then was sure. They were downwind of a fire, and it might not be far away.

She stopped, and the others caught up with her and smelled the smoke, too.

"How far?" Sheriff Kellerman asked.

Jessie shrugged. "Half mile, a mile. Let's go find it."

They worked ahead carefully now, trying to soften all of their movements. The valley bent to the left, and when they came around the small bend, they could see smoke ahead in a gentle layer where the winds hadn't reached it.

Behind the layer of smoke, the mountains rose up steeper, with a jagged section slanting up almost from the edge of the water. Jessie stared at the towering rock wall for several minutes, and those behind her came up and looked as well.

"I can't spot anybody up on the cliff," Kellerman said.

"Just can't tell where an outcropping might produce results," Jessie said. "Let's move on up but be quiet, and have your rifles ready. If you shoot, don't try to hit anyone. We should be able to overwhelm one man with our threat and our firepower."

They moved more cautiously the last half mile. Jessie pushed past an Indian paintbrush bush and looked across the stream. It had dwindled to half its size now. She saw smoke coming from a camp fire that was almost burned out. Near it were three bedrolls and a pioneer chair made out of a chunk of log.

No men were visible. The searchers stayed in the cover and watched the area. Jessie pointed to the right, up the chattering stream.

"Through the ferns beyond the fire. There's a trail of sorts. That could be the way they're going."

Jessie and her team crossed the stream as quietly as possible. Here the water didn't come over their boots. Then they moved farther into the brush and trees and worked their way upstream.

After a hundred yards, they could hear the sound of voices. Somebody laughed. A pick hit a hard rock with a clang.

They walked ahead cautiously. Ten yards later, through a

faint screen of snowberry bushes, Jessie saw the three men. Two of them worked at digging the start of a tunnel into the side of the cliff. They had removed a foot-thick-layer of dirt and hit hard rock. The third man sat on a rock, drinking from a canteen. He was the only one wearing a gun.

Jessie waited for her people to come up to her, then signaled that she would shoot, then they all were to bolt forward.

Jessie fired a round beside the gunman. He came upright in a reflex action, his hand reaching for his iron.

"Touch it and you're dead," Jessie shouted. Her rifle centered on his chest. Slowly he raised his hands.

The other two men lifted their hands, too.

Jessie ran toward them. "Do you men work for Starbuck Mining?"

"Glory be, we sure do," one of the men said. He was tall and thin. "I be Hal Ingels."

"My call name is Nehemiah Pope," the shorter man said. "It's hard to believe you're really here."

The sheriff took the outlaw's gun from leather and tied his hands together in front of him.

"It's good to meet both of you," Jessie said, shaking the hands of both prospectors. "I'm Jessie Starbuck."

"Glory be," Nehemiah said. "I figured we was slaves forever here. Never figured on seeing the outside world again."

Hal Ingels, the tall, thin prospector, took off his battered hat. "Miss Starbuck, we don't know for sure, but we think we found the mother lode here, at least one part of it. This place could be the biggest gold strike that Idaho has ever seen."

"That's great news. I'm glad we got here in time to help you. We've dismantled the Rooster's Nest. Chad Bannington is dead, swept down the river. Lunt Rockford slipped away on some Indian trails. But we've captured the rest of the outlaw crew."

"Glory be, I just never figured on seeing real people again," Nehemiah said. "God bless you, Miss Starbuck."

"Thank you. Now for another question. Do you know what happened to Page Dabrowski?"

"Sure as shooting do," Hal said. "Bannington shot him. First in the leg so he'd tell where the mother lode was. When Page wouldn't tell him, Bannington shot him in the side, and then when Page still wouldn't talk, Bannington murdered him with the head shot. Page never did tell him where the mother lode was. Bannington got roaring mad. Page could be stubborn, as you know."

Nehemiah nodded. "Page was a great man. He stood up to Bannington. All it got him was three bullets and a ride down the river. You find his body?"

"Down at the mill. We gave him a Christian burial."

"Glory be. Too bad, Page. I sure as blazes do miss that old coot."

Hal wiped his face and took a long breath. "We figured staying alive was more important than any gold mine, so we brought Bannington up here. We planned that we'd overpower him, but he tricked us and brought two men with him."

"Bannington paid the price for his last murder," Jessie said. She pointed to the start of the tunnel. "You don't have the right equipment for tunneling. You need some star drills, some eight-pound hammers, wheelbarrows, track, and timbers. Do you think this is the spot?"

Hal grinned. "If'n it ain't, then I'm a ring-tailed polecat. I swear this is where most of the yellow on this stream came from. Not a trace upstream, not one sparkle. Let me show you something."

Hal went to the side, moved some chokecherry bush branches, and brought out a handful of ore. He held it out for the others to see.

"White quartz gold, and look at the veining. Those veins are all pure gold. Quartz is the carrier. All we got to do is follow the quartz vein and mine our gold."

"You know that a hard-rock gold mine is a big investment," Jessie said. "Whatever the profits, you both get ten percent. We'll talk about it later. Do you both want to come back to town and rest up and sleep in a real bed and have some store-bought food?"

Hal shook his head. Nehemiah laughed. "No, Miss Starbuck. As for me, I'd sooner stay right here and dig on this tunnel. Would appreciate you sending us some equipment like you talked about and maybe hire us six men."

"What about supplies, food?" the sheriff asked.

"You blow up that shed up at the Nest?" Hal asked.

"No, we didn't even touch it."

"The place is full of canned and dry goods. Enough for the two of us to live on for a year."

"What about the placer mining downstream?" Sheriff Kellerman said. "Soon as we get back to town, the word is going to spread about the panning strike. There'll be two hundred men up here within a week."

Hal frowned. "Maybe we should drive us some stakes and then go down and file on our claims. Nehemiah gets two claims as discovery on the river, and I got one. Then Miss Starbuck claims the hard-rock mine in the company name. Best we do that first. Then we come back up here pronto."

They staked the hard-rock claim, stepping off five hundred feet one way and two hundred the other, for a rectangle that extended back into the mountain slope. They moved to the placer mining area, and Hal and Nehemiah conferred. At last they staked two claims a hundred feet long and running as wide as the canyon. Then they staked one more claim, Three Below, for Hal. They had covered all of the bend in the creek and several yards on each side of it.

"Why is the most gold here?" Jessie asked.

"This bend in the river is where the current slows enough so the gold can drop out of the flow," Hal said. "That makes this the best spot on the river. Be worthwhile gold up above and below, but the best is here."

Hal looked at one of the prisoners who had been panning gold. "Where are the leather bags, Jordan?" Hal asked him.

"Hell, right where you left them. I knew I'd never get any of the gold Bannington promised us. He'd kill us if we tried. He knew where it was."

Hal went to the edge of the stream and paced off twenty

long steps toward the woods. Then he turned right and went ten more paces to the base of a big fir tree. He knelt down and scratched away the leaf mold. A moment later, he found the first leather sack. It was eight inches long and three inches in diameter.

Soon he pulled three more from the cache. He took the four bags back and handed them to Jessie.

"This is what we've panned out here so far. I'd say we have about twenty percent of the gold that's in our three claims."

Jessie smiled and handed the bags of gold back.

"Hal and Nehemiah. This gold is yours. My agreement with Page was that any placer gold you found was yours to keep. If you found the mother lode, we'd do it in partnership. Ten percent for each finder, and the rest for the company. That agreement still stands."

"Glory, Miss Starbuck. There must be twenty pounds of gold dust here! At twenty dollars and sixty-seven cents an ounce, that's over six thousand dollars' worth."

"Good," Jessie said, smiling broadly. "Split it between yourselves, put it in the bank, and go back up there and see if our hard-rock mine is going to be a bonanza and really make you some money."

The deputies had the prisoners ready to travel. They hiked them down the trail until dark, then tied their feet and posted a guard over them.

The next day they pushed hard and got into Ruggins a little after five o'clock. Sheriff Kellerman sorted out the prisoners. He found wanted posters for all but two.

"I know you two are outlaws or you wouldn't have been up there in the Rooster's Nest. Only trouble is I don't have any charges against you, so I can't hold you. All I ask is that you get out of town fast—even if you have to walk."

The two hurried away from the sheriff's office and were last seen trying to raise enough money to buy horses and saddles for a trip back to Boise.

Sheriff Kellerman had told the prospectors before they got to town that the state land office in Ruggins was the place to register their claims and file on them. It had closed before they got there, and so had the bank.

The sheriff went to the bank owner and persuaded him to open for a special deposit. The banker smiled broadly when he saw the gold dust. He took out a seldom used scale and began weighing out the ounces of gold to figure the deposit.

By morning the word would be all over town. Gold up the Salmon!

Sheriff Kellerman established a checkpoint a half mile out of town, at the start of the river trail. He put up notices in the two saloons and at the general store that anyone going up the River of No Return must carry with him enough food to last for a month. Without a month's food, no prospector would be allowed up the river.

When asked why, the sheriff said he didn't want men killing one another up there for food.

"No handy cafes to stop by at and get a good meal," the sheriff told an audience in the Salmon Saloon that night. When the general store opened at seven the next morning, there was a line of forty men waiting to buy supplies.

Jessie had had a bath the previous night and a delicious sleep in the soft bed, and she woke up anxious to get on with the rest of the problem—tracking down the crazy man who had killed two of her mill hands.

She had breakfast with Ki, and together they hatched up a half dozen plans. None of them looked as if they would work.

Jessie turned to Ki and frowned. "Ki, we have to sit here until we come up with a plan that will work. We can't let this torturing, crazy killer get away with murder!"

★

Chapter 13

Jessie Starbuck sipped her coffee and stared over the cup's rim, out the window of the cafe on Ruggins's Main Street. She sifted back through all that had happened since they came to this small town just a few days ago. He had to be here. The killer had to be going about his normal activities and laughing at them.

Who was he? She knew a woman could do these crimes, but all the evidence she had pointed to a man, a madman.

"What about those men fired from the mill?" Jessie said to Ki, who sat opposite her. "Two of them are still in town, right? Brock Henshaw, who runs the general store and is getting rich off the new gold strike, and who was the other one?"

Ki put down his coffee and squinted his almond-shaped eyes. A moment later he nodded. "Garth Oberlin. He's the one you said was drunk when you talked to him in the morning, and exposed himself."

"He sounds crazy enough. Let's put a shadow on him and see what he does."

"My job," Ki said. "I had my run this morning. Felt good to get out and move after all that slow walking."

"You know where he lives?"

Ki nodded his head, so Jessie told him. "I'm going to talk with the sheriff again about this whole torture-murder situation.

131

There must be something we've overlooked."

They paid their check and went outside. Ki waved and headed up two blocks, to the cheaper side of the small town and the house where the schoolteacher's husband probably was drinking himself into an early morning stupor.

Ki spotted the house and meandered past on the far side of the street. It was just a dirt track between the houses, with only two homes on each side. This was out toward the end of the little village.

Ki saw that the house just across from Oberlin's was vacant. He walked out of sight, then circled around to the back of the vacant place and found the rear door unlocked. Inside, the house was empty of furniture. Ki looked out the front window and found a perfect view of the Oberlin house.

As he watched, a dog bounded out the front door and scurried around to the back. A minute later a man dressed only in long-john bottoms stormed after him. The man held a hatchet in one hand and a whiskey bottle in the other.

Ki frowned. Could a man who drank so much, starting in the morning, be coherent and clever enough to torture and kill two men and conceal his identity the way this killer had? Ki doubted this was their man. But he'd give it a good try. They had no better plan. This man and then Brock Henshaw. The general store man would probably shower them with more quotations from literature.

Ki had never heard of any of the quotations before, but he wasn't exactly a scholar of the printed word. He looked up and saw the man come back. He held the dog by one hand on the loose skin in back of his head and dragged him to the front porch. The man was Oberlin. He threatened the dog with the hatchet a few times, then kicked him and sent him howling around the house.

So much for kindness to animals. The man sat there on the porch, one hand on his genitals. He rubbed a bit, then got up and went inside.

Ki settled down to a long wait. It wasn't noon yet. Hard telling how many hours the man would stay in his house. Ki would be with him all day and night if he needed to be.

About that same time, downtown in the small courthouse, Jessie smiled at Sheriff Mark Kellerman. "You have a full jail, three men to a cell."

"Won't last long. I sent out letters to Oregon and California. Should be getting rid of most of them in two weeks." He frowned and touched her shoulder. "Hey, you look a little on the glum side. You found your two men alive and well. That must be a relief."

"It is, and the news about the gold panning and maybe a mother lode is great, but that doesn't help me find the killer you have roaming around your little town."

"True. I've been thinking about him, too. He's either damn clever or crazy, and maybe both. Yeah, probably both."

"I'd like to go over all the information we have on the two deaths. Everything. We must be missing something that's there in the reports and examinations. I want to do the whole thing again. Do you have a file on the cases?"

The sheriff pointed to two folders on his otherwise clean desk. "Exactly what I've been doing. I don't want to see another killing like these two."

"Ki and I have been battering our brains trying to come up with some new ways to find the killer. Not a lot of luck. We finally decided to put a watch on the two men who were fired, Oberlin and Henshaw."

"Oberlin is a no-good drunk, but he's never damaged anyone around here that anybody knows about. Henshaw is a pillar of the community and all that. So it still could be either of them or neither of them. You give up on Count Malenkov?"

"Ki talked to him. Said he was a blowhard but not dangerous."

"Might want to talk to him again. Two of the wanteds from the Rooster's Nest have asked the count to come see them. They claim he's their lawyer."

"How would they even know . . ."

"Right. They would have had to know him here in town before they went up the river. The count must have been a

133

contact man of some kind. Maybe him first, then the merchant, good old Brock Henshaw."

"Still, Mark, that doesn't tie him in with the twin killings here in town."

Sheriff Kellerman grinned. "Yep. Right. But it throws a different light on the man. Ruthie put him on her list. She might know more than she's told us."

Jessie stood and paced around the office. "Ki is watching Oberlin. Maybe it's time I had a talk with Ruthie, to see if she can help us a little more."

"Woman-to-woman talk?"

"Something like that. How is your one month of food rule going on the Salmon?"

"A few problems, but working out well enough. Brock Henshaw has sold out on flour, salt, oatmeal, and beans. He loves the idea."

"How many have gone upstream so far?"

"Through our checkpoint we had about eighty-five. I expect another hundred or so today. That path we took is going to look more like a highway before long."

"Keep them happy and we'll all get rich."

The sheriff waved, and Jessie went out of the office and down the boardwalk, to the house where Ruthie lived, on Cherry Street. She thought that particular street name was a put-on, but that's what it was named. It came right after Apple and before Prune Street.

Jessie knocked, waited, then knocked again. At last she turned the knob and pushed open the door.

Ruthie pranced into the hall and frowned at Jessie for a minute. Then she walked forward smiling. Ruthie wore only a fancy robe and slippers.

"You must be the rich lady from Texas. Jessie Starbuck. I've heard a lot of good things about you."

"Yes, I'm Jessie and you must be Ruthie. Ki has told me that you have your thumb on the heartbeat of this town."

Ruthie grinned, and Jessie saw a missing tooth on the side.

"I've been known to keep a secret or two."

134

"I'm hoping you don't have any secrets about the torture murders of my two mill hands."

Ruthie drew herself up as high as she could at five feet, shook her 250 pounds a moment, and stared up at Jessie. "Miss Starbuck, I might be a whore, but I'm not a liar, and I have nothing to do with any criminal conspiracy or anything like that. I told Ki I had no idea who killed those men. I gave him a couple of ideas, and that's as far as it goes with me."

"What about Count Malenkov?"

"He's a four-flushing son of a bitch I would walk a hundred miles to spit on. He used to be my pimp in Portland, and he does like little boys. Must be that he's scared each one he used so bad the kids are afraid to tell anybody about it."

"I've heard that happens. Was the count a contact for the outlaws here in town? Did they find him and then learn how they could go up to the Rooster's Nest?"

"Yes, but that's an entirely different matter. I saw some of the men he was with here and knew they were wanted. Does that make me an outlaw, too?"

Jessica shook her head. "Of course not. That situation is all resolved. But I still have to find out who killed my mill hands. Any more thoughts on it? Who is the craziest man in town?"

"Easy. Garth Oberlin. Crazy, but harmless. Gets wild out-of-his-mind drunk and runs around town shouting dirty words at prissy little old ladies who damn near bust their corsets and run home to change their wet bloomers. He could never kill anybody, let alone torture them."

"Any new suspects for me?"

"No. I have no more ideas." She leaned against the wall. "This killer has to be somebody usually as normal as anyone else, but now and then something sets him off and he goes wild. Could be anybody, even the sheriff himself."

Jessie laughed. "Ruthie, I kind of doubt that."

"Figured you would. He's one fine hunk of man, ain't he?"

"Indeed he is."

Ruthie scowled. "Could I ask you something personal?"

"Go ahead."

"I figure you're rolling him in the hay. So how does that make you so much different than me?"

Jessie sobered. "I knew a man once who said that all women were whores and all men were rapists. Some women traded their loving for money. Some women traded their loving for marriage and lifelong security. Some women traded their loving for being loved back for a few wonderful hours. So, you and I aren't a whole lot different. Just a matter of degrees."

Ruthie rubbed wetness from her eyes. "Thanks, Miss Starbuck. Nicest thing anybody said to me in a hell of a long time. I truly have no idea about who this killer is. I get any hints or ideas, I'll send you a note at the hotel."

Jessie thanked her and went back to the street and downtown. Another possible killer marked off the list. Ruthie seemed to think that the count should not be a suspect either. Ki would give her a report on Oberlin. In the meantime she had to come up with some new candidates. She sat at the Fir Cone Cafe and worked on a cup of coffee and a sandwich for lunch.

A half block down the street, Brock Henshaw raced around his general store, working harder than he had in years. There were ten men waiting outside the store, in a line that had grown and then reduced during the day.

All were looking for prospecting pans, tents, shovels, and food. First thing this morning, he had sold out on the three gold pans he'd had for four years. The shovels went next, and he never had any tents. Now it was food, the staples, and he was running low on most of them.

He had started to ration out what he had. More would come in by wagon from Boise in two days, but that wouldn't help now. On the stage out last night, he had sent an urgent request for more of everything to his wholesaler in Boise, after he heard the news of the gold strike and the food requirement for men going upriver.

A shot of whiskey would surely help him. He had never before drank when he was working, but this was a special case. Might not happen again in a century. He found the flask in the storeroom, where he hid it under some binder twine, and took a nip, then another. He put the flask back and hurried out to the front, to let in two more men who wanted to get rich panning gold.

Henshaw closed the doors that night at eight o'clock. There were still five men waiting to buy goods. He gave them numbers and told them they would be the first ones served the next morning. Then he went home and collapsed on the couch.

"We made more money today than we have in the past year," his wife said. She sat in an upholstered chair, her face strained and her whole body sagging with weariness.

"I hope it was worth it," Brock Henshaw said and turned over. "I'm going to have a little nap before it's bedtime."

The voices screaming in his head awoke him just before midnight. He sat up with a start. He groaned with the ache in his back from the unusual position he had slept in. Groggily he put his feet on the floor and stared at the wall.

The voices were pounding, pounding, pounding. He thought of the fresh bottle of whiskey he had hidden in the oats in the shed out back. Yes. Not many things could kill the voices. Sometimes the whiskey would do it.

A half hour later, he still sat in back of the shed, with the whiskey bottle in his lap. The alcohol hadn't dulled the shrill, driving, screaming voices one bit.

Tonight it was going to take human blood to wash away the sound.

Henshaw went onto the porch, took down his long black coat, and made sure the two pair of pliers were in it and the jar of coal oil. Then he walked quickly toward Main Street, angling down the alley just behind it. He stopped where the alley met Main and watched to see who would be passing by.

A few people were still moving about. He might catch one coming out of Ruthie's. Good idea. He detoured and found a spot to watch the whore's place. He knew it well. He liked women as fat as sin, and she was a good poking.

Two men came out about the same time and hurried down

the street. No chance for either of them.

Ten minutes later another man came out. Brock wasn't sure who he was. A drummer maybe from the hotel, pitching his goods and then moving on with the morning stage.

He walked a little unsteadily. The man was short and heavy. He struggled down the street and turned, so he would pass directly in front of where Henshaw waited in the shadows of the alley.

The merchant took out his six-inch knife and held it ready. When the man came to the alley, he hesitated, then hurried across it.

Henshaw pounced on him. His arm wrapped around the man's throat to cut off any cry, and Henshaw dragged him into the blackness. Henshaw drove the knife into the man's side, just over his belt and downward. A punishing wound that would hurt the man badly and take the fight out of him, but not one to kill unless it hit some of the intestines.

The man squalled in pain until Brock's hand covered his mouth. Brock dragged the man into the alley until he was almost at the middle. Some heavy cardboard boxes from the back door of a store lay there, and he moved them to make a shield. He smashed his fist into the drunk's jaw three times, until the stranger fell unconscious on the ground.

Brock dragged him into the shielded place and nodded. No time for a fire tonight. No branding. He took out the knife and sliced the upside-down crosses on the man's forehead. The cuts were deep enough to draw blood but not so it would pour out in a stream.

Henshaw made one cross on the man's cheek, but it bled too much.

What else? The voices kept screaming at him, beating him down, lifting the top of his skull with their incessant screeching and blathering.

The letting of the man's blood hadn't been enough. He had to do more. Like with the others. But he couldn't risk a fire here.

The pliers. He took them and held one pair in his hand.

What? How? He picked up the unconscious man's hand and used the pliers on the four fingers, mashing each one flat. More blood spurted from the four new wounds. The man groaned as each finger was mashed.

Brock smiled. The voices were fading. In a few minutes, they would be gone. He had a drink from the bottle he'd stuck in his coat pocket and nodded at the unconscious form on the ground. Then, just to make sure the voices stayed away, Brock drove his knife twice into the man's heart.

The victim twitched, his hands shook a moment, then he tried to sit up but flopped back and let out a long gush of air from his lungs. The man had ceased to exist.

Brock hurried home. He put the coat away on the porch, then slid back on the couch to finish out the night. It wasn't unusual for him to sleep on the couch. He slept there sometimes when his wife snored and when they had fights.

Brock Henshaw turned over, put his head on the pillow, and went to sleep within two minutes.

Earlier that same evening, Jessie had given up trying to find a new suspect, gone back to the hotel, ordered a bath, and luxuriated in it. She knew Ki was probably still watching Oberlin. She had no idea just where he had found a viewpoint, so she couldn't go and relieve him. She would take the job the next morning when he came in.

She was still tired from the trip up the Salmon. It was an early bedtime for her. For just a moment in bed she wondered what Mark Kellerman was doing, but she put that out of her mind. If she did any thinking at all, it had to be about the killer.

She solved that dilemma by dropping off to sleep.

In the house across the street from Garth Oberlin's place, Ki was still holding out. The man had chased the dog twice. He had come out on the porch naked once, evidently running away from someone inside.

He had remained inside most of the time after it grew dark. Lights blossomed in the house, and after a time all but one went out.

The last light stayed on. Now, about midnight, a figure came out the front door. It was Garth. Ki had tried the front door of his hideaway earlier and found it was unlocked and opened without any noise.

Now he let himself out of the vacant house and silently followed the big man down the dirt track toward Main Street. Was Garth the killer after all? Was he out on one of his murderous trips? Ki hoped so. He could catch him in the act of torture, before he killed, and have him wrapped up and all but on the platform for the hangman.

Ki hurried up the street after the hulking figure of Garth Oberlin, so he wouldn't lose him.

★

Chapter 14

Ki followed Garth Oberlin toward Main Street. Oberlin walked the best he could, with only a little staggering here and there and the inadvertent weaving of the normal drunk, but not yet in the falling-down class. Ki could never remember seeing Oberlin in either of the saloons in town. He must have been a solitary drinker.

Oberlin turned in at the first drinking emporium he came to, the Salmon Saloon. Ki went in right behind him. By the time Ki got inside the establishment, Oberlin was busy at the bar, counting out his change until he had twenty cents for a shot of whiskey.

The barkeep waited patiently for the money, then placed the full shot glass in front of Oberlin. The whiskey vanished in one swift gulp. Oberlin put the glass down and looked at the barkeep, who had walked away.

"One more," Oberlin said.

"Money?" the barkeep asked.

"On the house, for old times' sake. Be a friend."

The apron put the whiskey bottle under the counter and went to wait on someone else. Oberlin bleated in pain, stared at the barkeep for a minute, then looked around, evidently searching for a familiar face. He turned and made his way slowly to a table where two men played checkers.

Ki paid for a beer and watched the little drama. Oberlin talked to one of the men. The two checker players both laughed. Oberlin snarled something and took a swing at one man, but missed and fell across a neighboring table.

A minute later, a large man hurried up to Oberlin, helped him to stand, and then twisted his left arm behind his back and walked him out the front door. The bouncer came back, nodded at the apron, and continued to a back table, where he sat down.

Ki finished his beer and moved outside. For a moment, he couldn't find Oberlin. Then he saw him heading down Main Street toward the other bar. His mooching didn't pay off there either, but this time the barkeep grabbed him by the back of his shirt and his belt and levered him out the back door into the alley.

Ki asked where the outhouse was. The bar man pointed to the back door. Ki eased outside and found Oberlin sitting on a wooden box two doors down.

Ki walked that way, saw Oberlin, and went over and sat beside him. "You got a bottle?" Ki asked. Oberlin looked at him, a sneaky expression coming across his face.

"Maybe I got one, maybe not. You got one?"

"Nope, but I can get one. I got me a dollar."

"Bad whiskey costs two dollars a bottle," Oberlin said. "You got two dollars?"

"Maybe I do, maybe I don't," Ki said and laughed.

Oberlin watched him a moment, then he laughed. "I like you, a sneaky bastard like me. Hey, I got me fifty cents. You got a buck and a half? If you do, we buy a bottle and have a wild time smashing windows and tipping over buggies. What ya say?"

A half hour later, they had reduced the level of whiskey in the bottle considerably. They had already tipped over a buggy that had stood in front of a house up from Main Street. Now Oberlin raised the bottle again and smacked his lips.

"Best damn whiskey in the world. Know why? 'Cause I got it in my hand and then in my gullet!" Oberlin howled with laughter. He quieted long enough to take another huge drink and pass the bottle to Ki.

"Let's do something real mean and bad and dirty!" Oberlin shouted. "You feared of getting in a little trouble?"

Ki snorted. "These fancy little sheriff's deputies ain't gonna get me in no trouble. Smash them down in a minute."

"Good. Come on."

They walked down the street a short distance, then hurried past the side of a house to the backyard.

"Damn shit shed!" Oberlin whispered. "Let's tip the damn thing over on its side."

Ki lifted his brows. He'd heard of such pranks by juveniles around Halloween, but now?

Ki shrugged. "Hell, why not? You know who lives here?"

Oberlin shook his head. "Nope. We'll do three or four in a row and run like bastards!"

They tipped the first outhouse over. It landed with a crash, and a light blossomed in the back room of the house. They ran to the next place. That three-holer was harder to push over. They started it rocking, and at last it tilted and then crashed to the ground.

A shotgun blasted from somewhere behind them, and Ki heard the buckshot zinging past him. He ran away from the gunman, circled around, and made it back to Main Street. He had no idea where Oberlin was.

He slowed and walked to the Ruggins Inn, where he went up to his room. No sense in thinking that Oberlin could be a suspect in the murders. The man was a drunk, on the sneaky side, and he considered a dumb kid trick on someone to be a high point in his life. He'd rather tip over outhouses than murder someone.

Ki came to this conclusion as he did his nightly exercises and stretching. By the time he finished, he had decided he could report on Oberlin with complete confidence. The man was a mess, but he simply couldn't have tortured and then killed the two mill hands.

The next morning, Jessie and Ki had breakfast in the hotel dining room and were nearly finished when Sheriff Kellerman came in. He looked around, saw the pair, and headed for their table.

Jessie saw him coming and pulled out a chair for him. He

dropped into it and rubbed one hand over his face.

"You look tired, Sheriff. Hard night?"

"Yes," Kellerman said, not moving his hand. He pulled his hand away. "Our upside-down cross killer hit again last night. Did it in an alley right here in town. No branding, but the upside-down crosses were sliced into the man's forehead."

"Who?" Ki asked.

"That's part of the problem. The guy was a drummer out of Portland. Sold flatware and silver goods to merchants. He usually stayed one day, then took the stage the next morning. He missed the stage this morning."

"Not a mill hand?" Jessie asked.

"No, which breaks the pattern, which doesn't help us one whit."

"How did he do it?" Ki asked.

"Knife into the side was probably done first to take any fight out of the drummer. Some choking around the neck. Drug the victim from Main halfway down the alley, into some big cardboard boxes. Carved him up there, then stabbed him in the heart."

"Time of death?" Jessie asked.

"Doc wasn't sure. Figured around midnight to one A.M."

Ki caught Jessica's attention. "It couldn't have been Garth Oberlin. I was drinking and playing kid games with him in the dark until well after that time."

Jessie scowled. "No evidence at the scene?"

"Not a damn thing," Sheriff Kellerman said. "Not even any footprints, because a delivery rig went through there this morning before anyone found the body. It was hidden behind the boxes."

"So, it's another kill, but it doesn't help us any. I'm going back down to the mill. There must be something there that we don't know about, or saw and didn't recognize."

She started to get up, then sat down. "Mark, what do you know about the strange little person who calls himself the Birdman of Ruggins?"

"Birdman? He talk to you?"

"Told us he knew who killed the two mill hands. Said he saw it in a mystic vision. Claimed it was you. We left his place after I scolded him. What does he do around here? How does he make a living?"

"The birdman, a joke around town. Come to think of it, I have no idea how he survives. He doesn't have a job that I know of. He must have money he made somewhere else. He's never given me any trouble, so I don't bother him. No complaints about him."

Jessie nodded. "Figure I better check out everything. This is getting more complicated. Why would our killer switch from mill hands to a drummer?"

"Sounds more and more like the victims are random," Kellerman said. "Two were mill hands only because there are a lot of mill workers here in town."

Jessie stood. The two men popped up at once. "Maybe so, but I'm not accepting any of that until I can't prove it otherwise. I'm heading for the mill. Ki, you still look half-asleep. When did you get through with Oberlin?"

"About three this morning."

"So have another sleep until noon. By then I might know something more from the mill."

Jessie walked out of the dining room. Kellerman followed her. They paused on the boardwalk in front of the hotel.

"Dinner tonight at my place?"

She flashed him a pretty smile. "Maybe. If I can make some progress. This is starting to make me mad. Why can't we track down this killer?"

"We just haven't hit the key yet," Sheriff Kellerman said. "Let's hope we can find it before we have another victim."

They waved, and Jessie walked to the mill. It spread out along the side of the river, but used steam power to run the saws and chains and other lumber-working devices. The manager was in his office, set a good way from the whining of the big saws.

Elrod Grimp came to his feet the moment Jessie opened the door.

145

"Miss Starbuck. Good to have you here. What can I do for you?"

"Mr. Grimp. I'm looking for some kind of connection between the two men who were killed from your mill. What I need is a complete history of the men's records, where they worked, what jobs they did, who their immediate foremen were, what trouble they got into, reports on their work, all of that."

"Oh, well, that will take some time. We don't keep records on most of that. I can have our accountant go back over the pay sheets and give you those figures, which will help us place each man in an exact job.

"First with the sawyer, Zeek Young. He'll be easiest. He's been with the mill for almost ten years. Came up working half the jobs in the mill. He was bright, and I moved him into a spot where he could watch the sawyer. Then I put him on the slide rig, and then gave him a two-week training course with one of our sawyers."

"I'd like those records as soon as you can get them worked up. Was Young a foreman in any part of the mill before that?"

"Yes, several areas. He could do any job in the mill better than the man doing it. A fine person."

"Was he ever the foreman over any of those four men who were fired, the ones you showed me last time we talked?"

"Could have been."

"I'd like to be sure. Check your records and ask the men in the mill. I need to know if either of the men killed had been foremen of any of the four men laid off. You said Stone was on the green chain. That's tough work. I'd think that tough men would work there, who might get mad easily."

"True, Miss Starbuck. I'll check my records and talk to a number of the men who knew the dead men. They should be able to give us a good accounting whether or not the men fired had worked for either of them. I do know that Oberlin worked on the green chain for a while. So Stone would have been his foreman there."

Jessie wrote in her small notebook. "That's a help. Now I'll

146

get back to town and let you get this information together. I'll need it before supper tonight. Leave the material for me in my box at the Ruggins Inn."

Jessie stood and hurried out of the mill. Something bothered her, and she couldn't think what it was. About the mill, or the Birdman, or the count? She wasn't sure.

A half hour later, at the sheriff's office, she and Mark Kellerman had talked it through.

"I don't know why the Birdman makes himself out to be so weird," Sheriff Kellerman said. "Sure, he's got that shelter down by the river, but he also has a house up on Third Avenue, one of the nicest places in town. I've never been inside, but somebody said it had what they called fancy furniture, rugs, pictures on the wall, a real nice place."

"But he tells everyone he's Ruggins's Birdman. He has a real name?"

"Sure, figured you knew that. His legal moniker is Oliver Judd. But he won't answer to the name."

"Why would he search us out and then give Ki and me that wild story about his being mystical and that he saw you as the killer?"

"He's just weird. Everybody in town says he's just a little bit short of a full quart. He's strange and unusual, but harmless. I've never had a single complaint against him in my years here in town."

Jessie scowled. "Damn, I thought maybe we had something. Hoping he had something to do with the deaths and was putting on this big act for Ki and me to throw us off the scent."

"So what do we have left?"

"Not one great big batch of suspects. Brock Henshaw would still be a possible, I guess, since he was fired, but we've found nothing against him." Jessie stood and paced the room. She had on her cut-down jeans, a tight blue shirt with a blue neckerchief, and her flat-crowned brown hat, which she now let hang down her back by the chin strap.

"I'm tracking the work records of the two men fired from the mill and still in town. That might tell us something. Mr. Grimp

147

is also tracing back the work records of the dead men, to see if they had any foremen status over the suspects. But that's a wild shot in the sky hoping to hit a wandering Canadian goose."

The sheriff and Jessie met Ki for lunch at the cafe. He had slept and had a run and was anxious to get back to work.

"Ki, you did such a good job on Oberlin last night, tonight I want you to track our friend Brock Henshaw. He'll be working late at the store, so pick him up when he leaves there. He'll probably be so tired from making money that he'll go straight home and crash into his bed."

"Let's hope not," Ki said.

"How is the trek going up the Salmon?" Jessie asked.

"Smooth. About two hundred men up the river so far. Henshaw is about out of food. Gets in wagon loads tomorrow. So far none of the men have come back to file on a claim."

They ate toasted cheese sandwiches for lunch and then went outside, into the bright Idaho tall-sky country.

"I have one more errand to run," Jessie said. Sheriff Kellerman waved and headed back to his office. Ki decided to go to the general store and buy something so he could get a quick feel of the man he would shadow.

Jessie walked down Main Street to Cherry and knocked on Ruthie's door. She still wondered about the Birdman. Why such a charade?

Ruthie opened the door just as Jessie knocked.

"Saw you coming, hoped you wanted to see me." She eyed Jessie a minute. "Damn, but what I wouldn't give to have a sleek little sexy body like yours. Usually I don't mind being a fat cow, but goddam, you with that tiny waist and big boobs . . . Hell, I could get twenty bucks a throw at some fancy house in San Francisco if I was built like you."

Jessie grinned. "Not much of my doing, Ruthie. Just the way I happened to be. You have a couple of minutes to talk?"

"Damn! More sexy girl talk. Sure. Come on into my private quarters, then nobody will bother us."

Her special sitting room was about ten feet square, and feminine to the hilt, with lush print-covered chairs, a couch, fancy print pictures on the walls, a soft pink patterned wallpaper, and billowing pink curtains.

They sat, and Jessie got right to the point.

"What do you know about the Birdman, Oliver Judd?"

Ruthie laughed. "Now, there is a strange one. Every Sunday night, but don't ask me why on Sunday unless he's protesting. He wants something different every time and remembers if I try to repeat. He gets so sexed up he screams when he makes it. Strange, strange little man. But he's tender, never rushes or hits or calls me bad names. He's a gent even if he does have a little bitsy whanger."

"Have you been to his house?"

"The one at the river or the one up on Third? Yeah, I've done him both places. If he doesn't show up here by eleven o'clock, I go up to his place. He's always waiting."

"Any idea where he gets his money? So far all I've found out that he does is feed the birds down by the river."

"Yep. Says that's his full-time job. He's a nature freak. Loves the outdoors and birds and animals. Hates to eat meat because he knows some animal had to die. A real crazy."

"Is he rich from somewhere else or what?"

"He never talks about money. Says he has enough to last him. Always pays and tips me good. I got no complaints."

"You ever see anybody else up there at his place?"

"Well, not often. Once I saw a guy I was surprised by. Just as I was leaving, I saw the ever-loving Count Malenkov slipping out a side door. I didn't realize the two gents even knew one another."

The women talked for ten minutes more about Portland and San Francisco. Ruthie hadn't been there for ten years.

"I want to go back to that beautiful little city," Ruthie said. "I was born in San Francisco. Then my wonderful mother gave me away to her sister and we never saw mom again. Way it goes. I got out of my aunt's house as soon as I could. Had to rely on the one talent that I have."

Jessie steered her back to business. "Do you think there's any chance that the Birdman might be engaged in some kind of illegal activity to support himself? The Birdman thing could be just a disguise for his real money-making scheme."

"It just doesn't sound right to me, Jessie. But then I'm no big-shot university professor. What do I know?"

Jessie left shortly after that and was heading for the hotel when the little manager from the mill caught up with her.

"Miss Starbuck, been looking all over for you. Turned up one interesting fact in our study of our work assignments down at the mill.

"Three years ago, Brock Henshaw was a worker on the green lumber chain. One of the foremen he worked for on the green chain was the first man murdered, Will Stone. I had one complaint that Stone made about Henshaw, reporting that he did not work hard enough and that he had a bad attitude. Nothing ever came of it. Later Henshaw got moved to another job, but that report stayed in Henshaw's file and was one of the factors I looked at when I finally fired Henshaw."

"So, Henshaw might have hated Stone," Jessie said. "That's good. That's the first solid piece of evidence that we've had against anyone. Now he becomes more of a suspect. Anything about the sawyer Zeek Young?"

"Still working on that. But more than likely Zeek had been a lead man over Henshaw sometime in the five years Henshaw worked for us. Zeek bossed a lot of different areas of the mill. I'll get the rest of the investigation done on Zeek this afternoon."

Jessie nodded. "You do that. Any connection at all might be a help. Oh, don't mention this to anyone. We want everything to be done as quietly as possible."

Elrod Grimp nodded at his corporate boss and hurried away down the street, on his way back to the Starbuck Lumber Company's mill office. He had more work to do. The better he did it, he knew, the better his chances of continuing to be the general manager of the Starbuck mill.

★

Chapter 15

That afternoon, Ki bought some four-foot lengths of leather thongs at Brock Henshaw's general store. He had shopped for a while before he made his selection, and watched the retailer with a critical eye. He seemed as normal as applesauce and graham crackers.

Ki paid for the thongs and left the store. He checked out the rear of the place. Back there he found a small platform where heavy items could be loaded or unloaded from wagons. On the platform was a fifty-gallon drum filled with kerosine and some rolls of barbed wire, the small kind no more than a foot thick and containing a hundred yards of wire each.

He had found out where Henshaw's home was. It was closer to get there by going out the front door than the back, so Ki figured the merchant would use the front door when he closed for the night.

The store was almost out of staple foodstuffs. While Ki was there looking, two men came in for their hundred pounds of food to take up the Salmon. The place must have been swarming with prospectors by now. Ki was glad he wasn't up there.

He had a cup of coffee in a cafe, sitting at the window table so he could see the general store across the street. This would be his perch for the next few hours.

By three that afternoon, Ki had gotten restless, and he took a two-mile run out the north road, then came back to the same cafe, had a piece of pie and more coffee, and waited.

That night, the general store closed at six. Ki had seen Mrs. Henshaw leave at four, evidently to go home and get dinner for the pair.

Promptly at 6:05, Brock Henshaw left the store, locked it from the outside, and turned north, heading toward his house. Ki scowled. This might be a long night with nothing to do but sit and watch for the lights to go out in the Henshaw house.

During the supper hour, Ki hurried back to the cafe and ate a big bowl of beef stew, rolls, and coffee, and got back to the Henshaw place in a half hour. He hoped that Henshaw had not left the house.

It was still daylight. The sun wouldn't go down until nearly eight-thirty this time of year in central Idaho. Ki found a vantage point from where he could see into the Henshaw kitchen, and he was pleased to find both the store owners still at their supper.

Ki moved back to a vacant lot across the street from the Henshaws's and stepped behind a pair of six-foot Douglas fir trees. They were full with branches and completely concealed Ki when he sat behind them.

He folded his legs, then his arms, and lowered his chin toward his chest. He went into what he called one-eyed sleep. In this state, he closed one eye and half closed the other one, his breathing became deep and regular, and he willed his heartbeat to slow down.

He figured that ninety percent of his body was at total rest, as in sleep. Only one eye was awake and alert. It would warn him of any change in the house across the street, or if anyone left through the front door.

Nothing happened until dark. Then, with three lights still shining from the Henshaw windows, Ki saw the front door open. Brock stepped outside, turned, and said something to someone inside, then closed the door and went down the steps.

The moment he hit the ground off the steps, he turned and ran to the side of the house. Ki had to move to keep him in sight, and when he did, he saw the man enter his home's small back porch. Henshaw came out a moment later putting on a long black coat and a black low-crowned hat.

"Interesting," Ki murmured. He remembered what the crazy Birdman had said about his seeing a man in a long black coat kill one of the mill hands. Coincidence, or did this long black coat have any significance?

Ki figured half the men in town had coats like this. They were good to wear in the winter to ward off the rain and snow. Also good for bank robbers to hide sawed-off shotguns under. Ki watched as Brock Henshaw left his house and walked toward Main Street. The man wasn't going to a saloon for a casual drink. Twice Ki saw Henshaw stop, tilt a bottle and drink, then return the bottle to the pocket of his long black coat.

He hadn't pegged Henshaw as a drinker. The man had never been in any of the saloons Ki had visited. Maybe he was another secret drinker who exploded in violence when he got drunk enough. Maybe.

For a moment Ki lost the man, until he realized that Henshaw had ducked into an alley off Main Street. Was Henshaw stalking a victim?

Ki moved closer to the alley mouth, slipping along the boardwalk in the store shadows. He stopped six feet from the edge of the alley, in front of a stitchery shop. He could hear nothing. Two men and a woman came down the boardwalk, crossed the dirt of the alley, and continued past Ki on the boardwalk.

A lone man left the Salmon Saloon and walked toward Ki. He staggered when he stepped off the boardwalk, caught himself, and weaved as he worked back across it.

"Hey, hey you," a voice called from the depths of the dark alley. The drunk frowned, looked in the alley a moment, settled the six-gun on his hip, and walked on across.

Ki heard a long sigh come from the alley. A few moments later, Henshaw stepped out of the darkness and turned away from Ki, moving on down Main Street.

Had the try by Henshaw to trick the drunk into the dark alley been an attempt to lure a victim to his death? Or had it been a try to find somebody to drink with, or a hope that the man had a bottle of his own?

Ki wasn't sure. He tailed Henshaw. The merchant wandered up one side of Main and crossed over and worked down the other side. Once he stopped to talk to a falling-down drunk on the boardwalk. The man swore at Henshaw and he moved on.

Twice more Henshaw vanished into alleys and, it appeared, tried to entice someone in there with him. It didn't work either time.

A half hour later, he had wandered back to his house. Once there, he became more coordinated and sneaky. He slipped into the back porch and came out without the long black coat. Then he went to the front door, opened it, and walked inside.

Ki watched for another hour. The lights went out inside the Henshaw house. At that point, Ki slipped around to the back porch and tried to door. It was not locked. He opened the door and let the soft moonlight filter into the small area. Soon he could see the long black coat hanging on a hook near the inside door. He felt in the pockets.

The whiskey bottle wasn't there. In one pocket he found a pint jar filled with some kind of fluid. In the other pocket he found two pair of pliers. Pliers! What the killer could have used to make the brands.

Pliers had also been used by the killer on the fingers of the dead drummer.

Ki slid one pair of the pliers out of the pocket and carried them as he eased the door shut and started at a trot back toward Main Street. The pliers could be a real clue, if the print of the back of them could be matched up with the brands on the dead men.

When he came to the first light spilling from a saloon, he took out the pliers and looked at them. The jaws of the tool were blackened with soot, as if they had been held over an open fire to get them hot, hot enough to brand human flesh.

Ki nodded, excitement starting to grow. Then he grabbed his thoughts and turned them around. On the other hand the pliers could have become sooted holding a tin cup over a camp fire to boil coffee or getting tar hot for patching a

154

roof. Lots of ways. Best not to get overenthusiastic about this latest development. He would tell Jessie and the sheriff about it, however. Tomorrow.

Ki checked the stars. It was only a little bit after ten o'clock. A lot could happen after ten o'clock. Ki walked back to the Henshaw house and sat down behind the twin Douglas firs and then stretched out on his back. He could go on one-eyed watch and not miss a thing.

Ki left his watch post at one-thirty A.M. He decided that if Henshaw were going to go on another night stalking try, he would have done it by that time.

The next morning, Ki told Jessie what had happened with Henshaw. She wasn't impressed by Henshaw's fumbling attempts to stalk the drunks along Main Street.

"If he were the killer, I'd think he'd be a lot better at waylaying drunks than he seemed to be," Jessie said.

Ki told her about the soot-smudged pliers. He brought them out of his pocket and unwrapped them from a handkerchief.

"Well now, these are the pliers from his long black coat pocket?" Jessie asked.

"One pair of them. He had two."

Sheriff Kellerman, who had found them when they were almost through with breakfast, picked up the pliers and studied the jaws.

"The outside of the jaws here could have been used to make the brand marks on the two victims." He frowned. "The trouble is, ninety-eight percent of the pliers in town would also make that same burn mark."

Jessie nodded. "Still, it's more than we had. Now I'd say that Henshaw looks like our best suspect. He has the smoke-blackened pliers. He wears a long black coat and sneaks around the alleys at night, and he had been supervised and written up as a bad worker by Will Stone, who was murdered. That's more than we have on anyone else."

"But not enough to arrest the man for murder," Sheriff

Kellerman said. "Any frontier lawyer, even, would laugh us out of circuit court."

"Fine. We'll get some evidence you can work with. I'm going to see if I can find Mrs. Will Stone. There was something a little unsettling about our talk with her that first day we arrived. Like she was holding something back. She said she was working somewhere, Sheriff. Do you know where that is?"

"Heard she was cooking down at the cafe. We can go down and ask there."

"No. Thanks, but I think it'll be better if I talk to her alone."

"Fine, Jessie. I have some official things I should be doing anyway. This sheriff job would be fun if it didn't involve so much paperwork. Maybe we can have dinner tonight?"

Jessie nodded. "Maybe. Depends on what's happening. I've got a feeling this whole thing might be coming to a head sooner than we expect. I'll stop by your office after I talk with Mrs. Stone."

Jessie found Wanda Stone in the cafe. She was cooking, but this was the slow time of the morning. She and Jessie went out the back door, and Wanda lit a long, thin cigar. She grinned at Jessie's surprise.

"Will got me smoking them when he did. Claimed that we both might as well smell up the house. I got so I liked the taste, so I still smoke them." She took a long draw on the cigar and blew the smoke out.

"I've been expecting you, or the sheriff. I kind of figured you knew I didn't tell you all I knew that first day. I didn't know the lay of the land yet. Will hadn't been dead a month, and now this new one. Guess I was just plain scared."

"Having a husband killed would tend to upset anyone, Mrs. Stone."

She stubbed out the smoke and shook her head. "No, it was more than that. I really want you to find out who killed my husband and punish him. I'd do it myself, but I'm not a good shot, not even with a rifle. Will tried to teach me, but he said forget it. I could club a bear to death with a rifle faster than

156

shoot him. We used to do a lot of traipsing over the hills with packs on our backs. Went out for a week once. Didn't take a stick of victuals along. Lived off the land. It was the best week of my life. Will was good in the woods. Fishing and hunting, berries, roots, plants along the river."

"You really miss him, don't you, Mrs. Stone?"

"Please call me Wanda. Yes, I miss him, and even though he wasn't a perfect man, I wish I had him back. I want you to get the ones who killed him."

"Wanda, you said the ones who killed him. Do you mean you know that more than one person was involved in the death of your husband?"

She looked away. "Might have. Just a slip. I don't know. Sure Will got into some trouble before, but he was a good man. We all do little things we shouldn't sometimes. Still and all, Will was a fine husband."

Jessie stood and walked back and forth for a minute. Then she looked at the other woman. "Wanda, I think you know a lot more about this situation than you're telling me. I want to find the killer, too. I think the same man who killed your husband also murdered the other two men. Everything you can tell me or the sheriff will help."

Wanda held up her hands. "I've told you all of it. What more can I say? Right now I better get back to work if'n I want to keep my job. Come see me anytime."

With that, the woman went into the kitchen, where she had three orders waiting for her.

Jessie stared at her. Wanda Stone definitely knew more than she was telling. How could Jessie drag the truth out of her?

Back at the sheriff's office, Jessie told Mark Kellerman what Wanda Stone had said.

"She said two or three times that nobody was perfect, that Will might have done some bad things. Do you have any record on Will Stone before he was killed?"

"Can't remember them all. We keep some good records. Let's take a look."

Ten minutes later they found two items under William

Stone's name. He had been arrested once when he was nineteen for getting into a fight with a man over ownership of a horse. The matter was resolved, and Stone paid the man twenty dollars for the animal.

Three years later, Will Stone was arrested for stealing lumber from the local lumberyard run by the mill. He had backed a wagon up to the fence around the stacks of lumber and hauled off half enough to build a house while the guard on duty lay drunk in his shack.

A passerby had noticed the theft, followed Stone, and reported him to the sheriff. Stone, caught with the goods, confessed, returned the lumber, was laid off for a month from the mill without pay, and paid a fine of fifty dollars.

"So, looks like Will Stone was not pristine pure," Jessie said. "Was his old record what Wanda was talking about when she said he wasn't perfect? Or was it something he has done recently?"

"Nothing on the books about him for the past five years."

Jessie and the sheriff walked out to the street. "I want to talk to Ki about these new developments. Sometimes he can cut through the chaff and come up with the kernels of truth."

"What's that line across the street?" Sheriff Kellerman asked.

They walked over and looked at the men waiting to get into the Idaho State Land Office.

"Gold prospectors," Jessie said. They went up to the men and found them more than willing to talk.

"Yes, ma'am, I got me a sweet little claim. I'm Number Twelve Below on the Page Creek strike. That's twelve claims below the original one, and I have all sorts of color. I figure on it being worth at least a quarter a pan. I can't even guess how much my claim is gonna be worth!"

"How many claims staked now?" Sheriff Kellerman asked.

"I'm Thirty-One Below on Page Creek," a man down the line said. "Can't be many more below me, 'cause I'm almost to the Salmon."

"Lots of people up there?" the sheriff asked.

"About twice as many as can file claims. Gonna be some trouble before long. Wouldn't hurt to send a deputy up there to keep a little law and order."

Sheriff Kellerman nodded. "Might just do that."

Jessie and the sheriff walked down the street toward the hotel, talking as they went.

"We still planning on supper tonight?" Kellerman asked.

"I hope so. Pick me up at my room at six. If I'm not there, it's because something important on the case came up. You'll understand."

Jessie looked down the street and saw a man hurrying toward her. He was still fifty feet away and wasn't carrying a gun, but she tensed. Then she recognized the mill manager. He stopped in front of her and wiped sweat off his forehead.

"Glad I found you, Miss Starbuck. Located some more interesting material in my records."

Jessie grinned. "Take a minute to catch your breath, Mr. Grimp. I'm sure the news can be postponed for a little while."

"Thank you." He wheezed and gasped, wiped his forehead with a red handkerchief, and leaned against the storefront. He stuffed the cloth in his pocket and looked at Jessie.

"The last month before he was killed, Will Stone had been working two jobs at the mill and I knew nothing about it. He did his normal shift on the green chain, then worked from five to ten at night as a fire guard and night watchman. You know how sensitive a lumber mill is to fire, with all of the fuel around. Lots of mills burn to the ground, but we do a good job on fire patrol.

"We allow no smoking in the mill or the grounds, and have a constant watch on our burn pit, where we burn the slab wood and ends and junk wood and sawdust we can't sell. Have a screen over the top and keep the fire small so we don't have a lot of sparks flying."

"Yes, Mr. Grimp, your record on fire has been remarkable. But why is this important about Will Stone?"

"Goes to his moral fiber. He lied to somebody about himself to get the five-to-ten fire-watch shift. I don't know who hired him. I didn't. I'm looking into that. But don't you see, he's a liar, so maybe he was up to something else. I figured that you'd want to know, so I hustled right up here."

Jessie frowned. "Stone did have a police record for theft. Has the mill had any large-scale thefts of supplies or even lumber? Anything missing on a regular basis?"

"No, not at all. I keep close tabs on everything we buy. That would show up quickly in our cost picture."

"Well, thank you, Mr. Grimp, for this information. It's looking like Will Stone might not have been the most upstanding person after all. Anything new on Zeek Young?"

"Nothing, Miss Starbuck. I knew him best of any of the men at the mill. You won't find anything to tarnish his good name."

"Thanks again, Mr. Grimp. I'll be talking to you soon."

The mill manager nodded, put on his hat, and walked away down the street.

"Big news?" Sheriff Kellerman asked.

"What do you think? If there had been wholesale vanishing of goods or supplies from the mill, it might be important. Kind of like hiring a fox to guard the chicken coop. But if there are no missing chickens, I guess we can file that notice and forget it."

They parted, still with a tentative date for supper. Jessica went back to the hotel and found Ki waiting for her in the lobby. She brought him up to date on what the mill man had said about Will Stone.

"So we have one more stick for the fire under Henshaw. I've about decided we need to set up a trap for this killer.

"I want you to rest up this afternoon, Ki. As soon as it gets dark, I want you to be a stumbling-around drunk walking Main Street trying to get attacked by our homicidal maniac. Sound like a good part for you to play?"

160

★

Chapter 16

They met at the sheriff's office just before dusk. Ki was there with a shirt on, his town pants, and real boots. Jessie had her .38 revolver in leather on her right hip. Sheriff Kellerman wore a sidearm and carried a shotgun.

"Ki, one of us will be in sight of you all the time," Sheriff Kellerman said. "I've got two deputies posted on roofs at the sides of the saloons. Jessie and I will be in doorways, out of sight but watching you, Jessie on one side of the street, me on the other."

Jessie frowned at Ki. "I'm not sure this was such a good idea I had. Maybe we should cancel it."

"Not a chance," Ki said. "I can play a drunk as good as anybody. I've had experience. If this will nail down the killer, that's great. Just so we get him taken care of before he does me in."

"You promise not to wait too long before you go on the offensive," Jessie said. "I don't want you getting hurt."

"Nobody using a knife and a pair of pliers can hurt me. Especially not when I'm waiting for him to try. I'll be fine. I'll be half-sloshed when I go into the first saloon. Have a beer and weave my way out and start working the boardwalks, going slow past the alley openings. If I don't strike fire there, I'll hit another saloon and repeat the act."

Jessie's frown was still there. "Maybe we should cancel the

161

whole idea. What do you think, Sheriff?"

"Best way to trap this killer is with bait. I don't think we have anything to worry about. My only worry is that we're starting too early. This guy must work late at night. Let's put a hold on this until ten o'clock."

Ki shrugged. Jessie nodded. "Yes, ten o'clock sounds good. Then we can run the test for two hours, and Ki won't really get drunk."

"I never get drunk."

Jessie patted his shoulder. "I know, and it's still a good line. Anybody have cards? We could have ourselves a good game of poker."

"In the sheriff's office?" Kellerman asked, feigning shock.

Two hours later, Ki had won almost the whole box of large kitchen matches.

"Let's see, that's about four thousand dollars that each of you owe me," Ki said.

"Put it on my tab," the sheriff said. "We about ready?"

"Anytime you are," Ki said.

Kellerman sent his two deputies out to climb up the back of the saloons so they could be in position when Ki began his rounds.

Before they left the office, Jessie backed Ki against the wall with her finger punching his chest. "Ki, I want you to promise me that you'll be careful. If we make a contact, he's going to be surprised, then desperate and deadly. He might have a hideout."

Ki grinned. "Yes, Mother," he said, and Jessie had to laugh with him.

Five minutes later, Ki strolled down the boardwalk and went into the Salmon Saloon, the best one in town. Sheriff Kellerman had gone ahead and slipped into the eight-foot-deep V entryway of the Diamond Drug and Pharmacy. Earlier, Jessie had walked up the dark street and, when no one was looking, slid into the doorway of the general store.

She was beyond Kellerman. He was two doors from the alley going north from the Salmon Saloon. The men on the roofs of the two saloons each had a rifle, but had been instructed not to shoot to kill. They wanted this man alive.

Jessie leaned against the wall of the entryway and took three deep breaths. In a way she hoped that nothing happened. On the other hand, if they could get the killer to attack Ki with a knife and drag him into an alley, it would be a simple matter for Ki to overpower him and capture the man.

For five minutes she watched the street from the very edge of the entryway. Three men came by singly. All moved past at the outside of the boardwalk, especially at the alley. Each man seemed to be alert, watched the alley carefully, then hurried on past.

Jessie gasped. She had just looked around the edge of the building and seen Ki coming. He was close to the buildings, which would put him almost in the shadow of the alley when he passed.

Ki was three doors down. The alley was two doors the other way. Ki came on and soon was at Jessie's building. He staggered, leaned against the wall only inches from her and grinned.

"How'm I doing?" he whispered. Before she could answer, he chuckled and staggered away. He stepped down from the boardwalk to the dirt of the alley, doing it in an elaborate way, as if to prove he wasn't drunk. Then he stumbled and staggered into the alley a moment, and Jessie caught her breath.

In a few seconds more, Ki staggered back out of the alley darkness, continued to the other side, and stepped on the boardwalk. He moved slowly toward the next saloon. He had passed her alley and one dark, narrow street up a ways. So far so good.

Four more times that night, Ki made his trek up and down the boardwalks. He should have become progressively drunker, but he told Jessie once when he leaned against her building that if he got any drunker, he'd have to fall down and pass out.

Jessie watched him come for the sixth time. She heard something and looked to her right and saw a figure leave the boardwalk and ease into the alley. Was it the killer?

She hoped Ki would lean against the wall next to her hideout this time. She could warn him that someone was there. She could see Ki three doors away, coming toward her. How could she warn him?

He came closer, almost fell, then was past her spot, and she had no chance to talk to him. She drew her gun, came out of her hiding spot, and trailed Ki, twenty feet behind. He looked back once when he heard her footfalls. She made them softer. He shrugged and stepped off the edge of the boardwalk into the dirt. He staggered again, slipped half into the alley dark, then came out and sat down on the edge of the boardwalk, his feet in the dirt.

A moment later another figure came out of the alley. Jessie raised her six-gun. The figure was a man. He swayed in the dim light from the moon. Then he took a step toward Ki.

The man had worn clothes that looked dirty and ragged. His beard was long and matted. He motioned to Ki, who watched him with a sharp eye.

"Hey, buddy. You got a bottle? I'm fresh gone from my money. Sure as hell need a drink. You got a bottle?"

Jessie relaxed and pushed against the front of the store. Ki shook his head at the drunk. "Hey, buddy, I got no money, got no bottle. Hoped maybe you had a couple of swallows left in a pint."

"Damn no."

"Anybody left in the saloon?"

"Threw me out."

"Me, too," Ki said.

The drunk shrugged and took two steps down the boardwalk.

"Where you going?" Ki asked.

"Livery. Guy there lets me use a vacant stall, if'n I clean out a few in the morning. Damn tired." The drunk plodded on, forward down the planks in front of the stores, heading for the livery at the north end of town.

Ki turned and watched him go. When the drunk faded into the darkness of the night, Ki walked back to where Jessie stood frozen against the front of a lawyer's office.

"I think we struck out on this one, Coach," he said. They had seen two baseball games recently, and Ki had taken to the game at once.

Jessie watched him, then touched his shoulder. "Are you all right?"

"Fine. Just no killers roaming the streets tonight. I'd like to get a little sleep for a change."

"Agreed." They walked off to where Sheriff Kellerman leaned against the wall of the entryway.

"Ki thinks the game is over for tonight, Sheriff," Jessie said.

"I say he's right. It would have been too easy this way. Let's call it a missed opportunity."

Sheriff Kellerman whistled, and the two deputies on the saloon roofs whistled back. They were coming down.

"Nothing?" Kellerman asked.

"A whole lot of nothing. Had one chance in the alley up there, but he turned out to be drunker than I was and tried to mooch off me."

"So we try something else tomorrow," Kellerman said. They headed back to the hotel. Jessie stopped.

"Ki, breakfast at the hotel as usual, seven A.M.?"

"I'll be there, if I can sleep that long."

Jessie caught the sheriff's hand. They went to his office, where he told the special rooftop men to go home and checked with the duty deputy. All was quiet.

A half hour later Jessie lay contentedly against the large, naked body of Sheriff Kellerman in his big bed.

"This could get to be a wonderful habit," she said.

"I keep telling you to throw over that business of yours and come cook and wash for me and raise babies with me here in Ruggins."

She turned to face him and leaned up on one elbow, with her hand under her head, letting her coppery-blond hair fall down over her elbow and the pillow. "Sometimes I wish I could do just that. The trouble is I've got responsibilities. People depend on you to keep the law and order in your county. A whole lot of folks depend on me to keep their jobs going and

165

their lives on track. But sometimes . . ."

She moved over and kissed him gently, then snuggled against him. "Right now I just want you to hold me and not let me go until the sun comes up."

The next morning, after breakfast at the hotel, Jessie and Ki both went to talk to Mrs. Wanda Stone. She wasn't at the cafe where she usually cooked. Ki asked the waitress where she was.

"Oh, yeah, Wanda. She sent word that she couldn't make it in today. She said she was sick, too sick to cook."

Ki and Jessie walked out to the woman's house. Ki knocked three times on the door before she came. She had dressed, but her hair was a mess and her face showed the blotches of late sleep.

Wanda stumbled a little as she let them in. She shook her head and squinted at them.

"What a head I have. Okay, so I drank a little last night. Maybe I should have known all along."

"You found out who killed your husband?" Jessica asked.

Wanda lifted her brows and then squinted her eyes. She rubbed her forehead and leaned against the wall. Three times she pounded the wall with her fist, then she tried to relax.

Wanda dropped on a sagging sofa and waved them to chairs. "No, I didn't find out who it was. Found out some other things, though."

"Like what, Wanda?"

"No business of yours. But now I want Will's killer more than ever."

"Wanda, I looked up your husband in the sheriff's records. Turns out he was arrested twice. Once for theft. He stole a whole wagon load of wood and lumber from the mill's lumberyard."

"Five years ago. He paid his fine."

"We also know that Will was working two jobs at the mill. The second one as a fire guard and watchman on the five-to-ten shift, under another name."

166

"Found that out, did you? How will that help you find who killed Will?"

"Never can tell, Wanda. You kept saying that Will wasn't perfect the time we talked before. I'll say he wasn't perfect. You know that he'd been stealing goods and tools and material from the mill during his watchman duties, don't you?"

"What?"

Jessie had taken a chance. It was a possibility. If he had been stealing late at night, it might open up some new reasons why he was killed. She watched Wanda react.

"Don't know nothing about that. Nothing!"

"Wanda. We both know it's true. I'm getting a search warrant to go through your place here, including that old barn down by the wagon. A perfect setup. Shall we go down there now and look around?"

"No, you can't. I mean there's nothing to see. Oh, damn!" Wanda stared out the window, then the tears came, and she wept into her hands, then against the sofa back, and after five minutes, she turned to Jessie.

"He's my husband. I got to stand by him."

"You want to find out who killed him, help us on this. Will didn't do this alone. He had to sell the goods to somebody. Let's go take a look in the old barn."

Ki looked at Jessie, who nodded and motioned him ahead. They hadn't talked about this theft angle. Jessie had thought of it as they walked up to the house. Will was a convicted thief. What would be more natural than for him to continue his ways? The night watchman job gave him the perfect chance to steal material and get it out of the mill without being questioned.

The theory was good. Jessie hoped it held up now that she was putting it to the test.

The barn had been used as a barn early on. Now it was only a store shed. Big double doors creaked as Ki pulled them apart. Tall enough to drive a team through. On each side of the center were grain bins that had been added later. A big pile of hay still filled one bin, and to the back were two cow stalls waiting for the morning milking—if Mrs. Stone had had a cow.

An old dusty tarp covered something in the second bin. A solid wall had been built up four feet on all the grain bins, and sections could be nailed on above that to contain shelled corn or threshed wheat or other grain.

Ki vaulted over the wall and lifted the tarp. Jessie grinned. Ki folded back the canvas and laughed softly. Wanda Stone gasped.

"Oh, my! I never dreamed he had so many things in here."

Jessie quickly evaluated the stored loot. There were a dozen falling axes, half a dozen six-foot cross-cut saws, boxes filled with files, three cases of dynamite, and half a dozen boxes that didn't show what was in them. To one side were dozens of new wrenches and tools.

"Not the sort of thing that a big mill operation like mine would miss if they were taken a few at a time," Jessie said. She turned to Wanda, her eyes sparking fire now.

"Wanda, you knew about this, knew about the stealing from the mill. You knew, didn't you?"

Wanda sighed and leaned against the bin wall. "Yes, I knew he was bringing a few things home at night. He never told me what or how many."

Jessie stood in front of Wanda, her fists on her hips. "So you knew about it. You also must know who he worked with and who he sold the merchandise to."

Wanda looked around, shivered slightly, then nodded. Her voice was so soft Jessie could barely hear it.

"Yes, I know." She sighed. "I just want to punish the man who tortured and killed my husband. Is that such a bad thing?"

"Not at all. I want to find out who he is as well."

"They came to Will with the idea. We had been doing fine. I had the job and he had a job, and we rented this place after old Mr. Kirkpatric died. We were thinking of getting our family started. Will was over his wild phase. He was straight and true until they started pushing him."

"Who are 'they,' Mrs. Stone?"

She went on as if she hadn't heard the question. "They said it would be easy. All Will had to do was get a job as night watchman for a couple of months. They said they could arrange it and use another name, and the manager would never know.

"I guess the thrill of it, and the chance to make some extra money, was too much for Will. He didn't even tell me about it. Just got the new job and started working, and now and then I'd see him drive home in a wagon with a second little man helping him. They unloaded things in the barn, and then the little man drove off with the wagon.

"When I asked Will about it, he wouldn't tell me a thing. Then at last he told me about it."

"Who was the little man who drove the wagon, Wanda?" Ki asked sharply.

She looked up, jolted out of her memories.

"Oh, the little man was the one they call the Birdman. I think his real name is Oliver Judd. It was his wagon, and he set up the whole thing."

Jessie nodded. "What happened after that?"

"Once a week they would drive here at midnight, load some more things on the wagon from the barn, and drive away. It was three weeks before Will told me that they sold the things to the general store, to Brock Henshaw. There was no way any of the items could be traced back to the mill. Fact is a lot of the material had been bought at the store in the first place.

"One night Will came home. He'd been drinking, and he was happier than I've ever seen him. He showed me a roll of paper money. He said he had over two hundred dollars. That was his share. He said there would be lots more. Two hundred dollars is more than Will makes in six months' work at your mill."

"So the Birdman and Brock Henshaw were in on the theft ring," Jessie said. "I don't see how that shows us who killed your husband."

"Oh, I'm not through. Will was so pleased to be making all

169

this money, that he figured out how he could make even more. One night, he rented a wagon, and that night he brought things home himself, without the Birdman. He laughed and danced and said now we could do better than ever. The middle man was out of the picture. Now Will would steal the things and keep them here for a while, then sell a batch to Henshaw. He wouldn't have to split the money with the Birdman."

"Did the Birdman find out about it and kill your husband?" Jessie asked.

"Will sold to Henshaw by himself just once. Henshaw wasn't happy about it. I think he told the Birdman. Judd, the Birdman, came to see Will one night real late. Said they had to talk. They went for a walk. Will never came home. It was the last time I saw him alive. When they found him dead, I hid all the cash we had, even the dirty money from the stolen goods."

Jessie took Wanda's hand and and led her out of the barn. Ki covered the goods with the tarp and followed them.

Back in the kitchen, Ki started a fire in the stove and put on coffee to boil.

Jessie and Wanda sat down on the sofa, and Wanda went on with no prompting.

"I know Birdman had something to do with Will's murder. But he's not strong enough to do it himself. Figure Brock Henshaw helped him. The branding is the key. We had Brock over for supper one night when they were planning the whole theft scheme. Brock was a little drunk, and suddenly he began to rub his head. He jumped up and ran around bellowing in pain.

"He yelled that there were demons screaming in his head. He saw our old dog, and he ran at it with his knife. His eyes were wild; he was drooling and screaming. He killed old Max, our mixed-breed dog, and then knelt by the dog and washed his hands and his arms in the blood.

"Then it was over. He stood, looked at his bloody arms and hands, and went to the creek and washed it all off. He came back and apologized for the dog, gave Will ten dollars for it, and promised to get us another one. He gave us no explanation.

170

They had been drinking after supper, but he just exploded all at once.

"I'd guess that Birdman went to see Henshaw, or Henshaw had him outside waiting, and Henshaw went into one of his wild times and wound up torturing Will and then killing him. One could hold a gun on Will and the other one tie him up. Wouldn't be hard, two on one that way."

Jessie stood and walked back and forth in front of the sofa. "What you say is probably true, about Henshaw killing Will. The trouble is, Wanda, we have no proof. Will you testify in court that you saw the Birdman bringing stolen material to your barn, and then loading more stolen goods into your wagon?"

"Testify, in court? Sure, if that'll help you catch Will's killers."

"It will. Now we have some work to do. Wanda, don't tell this story to anyone else, do you understand?"

"I won't tell it to nobody, unless you say to. I'll go back to work tomorrow. Work is best; it stops me from thinking about Will too much."

Jessie thanked Wanda, and they left before the coffee was ready. They walked straight down to the small courthouse and Sheriff Kellerman.

Jessie told him what Wanda Stone had related. The sheriff nodded and filled out a paper charging the Birdman with theft, receiving stolen goods, and the sale of those goods. One of his deputies grinned, took the paper, and hurried out the door.

"We'll have the Birdman in his own private bird cage before long," Kellerman said. He sat down at his desk and covered his face with both hands.

When he looked up, his face was grim. "The big problem is we know Henshaw and Birdman killed Will Stone, and probably the other ones as well, but we don't have any proof."

"Wanda said Henshaw was nervous and worried when he talked to Will that time he went crazy," Jessie said. "He'd also been drinking a lot. Maybe we can set up the same set of conditions for Henshaw and set him off again."

171

Ki looked at Jessie. "Conditions? I can find an excuse to get him drunk. That's no problem."

"What would make him nervous and angry?" Kellerman asked.

Ki suddenly laughed. "I've got the solution to that problem, too. It will take some setting up, but I'd guess we can do it tonight. We get him wild crazy and turn him loose, right?"

Sheriff Kellerman nodded. "Then we use two of my deputies to pose as drunks wandering the town like Ki did last night. He grabs one of them and attacks him, and we have enough proof to convict the man. With any good luck at all, we can get Birdman to turn state's evidence for a lesser sentence."

Jessie eyed Ki with a sly grin. "So, wonder worker Ki, just what kind of plan do you have in mind to turn Brock Henshaw into a raving maniac?"

★
Chapter 17

Ki outlined his plan, and both Sheriff Kellerman and Jessie chuckled over it.

"Should work," the sheriff said. "A trick like that would make me powerful angry."

Jessie laughed. "You men, you are shameless. Sometimes I don't understand you." She looked at the sheriff then and grinned. "Then sometimes I understand how you think all too well."

A disturbance at the back of the jail brought the sheriff out of his chair and rushing back there. He returned a few minutes later laughing.

"Well, we have the Birdman safely in his new cage. He doesn't like it. Wanted him brought in the back way so nobody would know about it. We keep it all quiet until after tonight, and maybe we'll have both of them."

"I see you made some room by shipping out some of your Rooster's Nest inmates," Ki said.

"Three went out on the morning stage heading for Oregon. One left yesterday for Boise. I've made a lot of friends with that capture up there. I want to thank both of you."

They nodded. Ki stood. "Well, I better have a big lunch and then get a nap before my grueling workout tonight." He shook his head. "Sometimes it's surprising even to me the lengths I go to just for the cause of justice."

Jessie threw a wad of paper at him, and they all laughed

as the pair of Texans left the office.

"I'm on my way out to see the mill manager," Jessie said. "It's time he put in better controls on the use and replacement of small tools, files, axes, and other expendable supplies. I'll tell him about how he's lost at least two thousand dollars' worth of equipment in the last two months."

They had lunch, then Ki went on a conditioning run.

"Five miles will be about right, then a nap before I go into the general store and become a long lost friend of Brock Henshaw."

"How will you do that?"

"Just work it as it falls, take it as it comes, play it by ear, all that sort of thing. Improvise. I'll figure out something. He's a literature nut, that doesn't help me any. I'll try to get him to come with me right after he closes up his store. He doesn't drink in public, so it'll be with our own bottle. I'll do a lot of spitting out when I use the bottle, or just not swallow any. Lots of ways."

Jessie had a two-hour session with mill manager Elrod Grimp. She told him about the thefts, and he was shaken. She told Grimp that he needed to establish new rules, that whenever an item was used up or broken, it must be turned in before a new one could be issued.

They set up a new worker who was responsible for tools, equipment, and supplies, and he was given absolute authority over the goods. He would turn in an inventory each month of tools and equipment broken and scrapped, new ones issued, and what orders were placed for needed items.

When Jessie had this all in place, she smiled at Grimp. "Outside of this one little leak, you've been doing a good job here, Mr. Grimp. I have no thoughts of replacing you, so just relax. You have a good way with the men, they work for you, and you get the production we need. So keep it up."

Jessie smiled when she saw the look of relief that came over the manager. She told him not to mention the thefts to anyone, not even the new man he had selected to control the small goods. Then she went back to the hotel.

If all went well tonight, they could have the problem solved by midnight.

At a little before five o'clock that afternoon, Ki hurried into the Ruggins general store and checked the counter where the knives were displayed. He had been wanting a small penknife, the single-bladed knife with a cutting edge no more than two inches long that could be honed incredibly sharp.

He knew that Mrs. Henshaw would be home by now. Brock himself came up and nodded.

"Something in the way of a good penknife today, sir?"

"Yes. Been wanting one for a long time. Emergency kind of blade no man should be without, even though I don't trim quill pens much anymore."

Henshaw chuckled. "I like a man with a good sense of humor. The bard, Mr. Shakespeare, said it well in *The Merchant of Venice*: 'Nature hath framed strange fellows in her time, Some that will evermore peep through their eyes and laugh like parrots at a bagpipers.'"

"Excellent, Mr. Henshaw. Coming from Japan, as you may have noticed, I had little training in the great English bard. However, we have some Japanese writers who are quite well known and just as profound. Have you heard of Santo Yamaguchi, from the sixteenth century? He said in one of his formal essays: 'To laugh is joy, to cry forbidden, as the sun rises, so shall joy rise with you if you can laugh.'"

Henshaw nodded slowly. "Yes, yes, I can see the structure of it. Would you mind repeating that so I can write it down? I read a lot of literature, love it. I'll always remember that part about joy rising with the sun. By damn, it's a good reason to get up in the morning."

He had Ki repeat the words. Ki struggled to remember what he had said, but together they pieced it into its proper form.

Ki bought the knife and paid for it, then tarried. "Do you have any more quotes from this Shakespeare fellow? He sounds like a man I would like to read more of."

Henshaw smiled. "Sir, I have a library full of him. Twenty-seven books I have of his plays and poems. Everything I can find about him. Many of them come from England by special order through one of the largest booksellers in New York. If you have time, I'd love to show my collection to you."

"It would be my pleasure."

Henshaw checked the store and found no customers, so he took Ki back to his small office against the far wall of the storeroom. He waved at a shelf filled only with Shakespeare's works, just over his desk.

"These books are my children, my lovers, my wonders. Simply, my joy. I'm afraid I'm misplaced out here in the wilderness. I should be at some great university teaching the bard to a new generation of scholars."

"You said your joy. This fellow Shakespeare is your joy?"

"Amen and amen. He is. William Shakespeare, an Englishman now long dead, but his prose and poetry will live forever. Might I read you one of my favorites? I'm memorizing it but haven't got it well done yet."

Ki nodded, and the man reached for a worn volume and opened it to a marked page. "This is from *A Midsummer Night's Dream*.

" 'The lunatic, the lover and the poet,
Are of imagination all compact:
One sees more devils than vast hell can hold,
That is, the madman; the lover, all as frantic,
Sees Helen's beauty in a brow of Egypt;
The poet's eye, in a fine frenzy rolling,
Doth glance from heaven to earth, from earth to heaven,
And, as imagination bodies forth
The forms of things unknown, the poet's pen
Turns them to shapes, and gives to airy nothing
A local habitation and a name.
Such tricks hath strong imagination,
That, if it would but apprehend some joy,
It comprehends some bringer of that joy;

176

Or in the night, imagining some fear,
How easy is a bush supposed a bear!' "

Ki stood there a moment, not following it, but lulled along by the meter, the sound of it.

He nodded, trying to look impressed. "Yes, my friend, you are indeed buried here in the wilderness. To make up a bit for your fate, could I take you to dinner tonight, and we can talk of writers and poets to our heart's content."

"Done and done again, to quote the Bard. I'd be delighted. I'll close the store at six, hurry home and tell my wife of my good fortune, and meet you at your convenience."

"Say seven o'clock at the hotel's dining room. They have the best food in town."

"Done and done again!"

Ten minutes later, Ki reported his appointment with the literary side of Brock Henshaw to Jessie.

"He suspects nothing?"

"Not as long as I come up with more phoney quotations from that ancient Japanese poet Yamaguchi."

"Is there such a man?"

"Not that I know of. But Henshaw doesn't know that. I'll have a flask of whiskey along for dinner, and we can lace our coffee with the potion. Get him started. Then an hour in the dark with our bottle of whiskey, and he'll be more than ready."

"You still think it'll work?"

"As near to a signed contract as I can give you. She told me that she'd seen him before, so it won't be anything new."

It all went as Ki had figured. The dinner was delicious, the whiskey coffee got Henshaw started. An hour later, outside, they finished the bottle and Ki suggested they visit Ruthie.

"I need a good woman," Ki said.

"Hell, I ain't poked Ruthie in a month," Henshaw said. "Let's go."

Ruthie had been briefed that afternoon and had everything arranged. When they had gone in her Cherry Street door, she hung out the "Sorry, busy" sign and locked the door. She took them both up to the double bedroom and at once whipped off her robe to reveal her pink, gloriously fat, naked body.

Henshaw roared in delight and grabbed one of her huge sagging breasts.

"Hot damn, tits! More tits than I ever saw in my goddam life. Me first, you sexy little lady. Hell, I'm hard as a railroad spike already!"

She pushed his hands away and shook her head. "Not a chance. You calm down a little. You might hurt yourself. I'm taking on the Japo here first. He's got a wild whanger, Oriental style, if you know what I mean."

Ruthie played it just the way Ki had told her to. She lay down on one of the big beds and held out her arms. Ki dropped on top of her, and she began taking off his clothes.

"What the hell am I supposed to do?" Henshaw yelped.

"Hell, watch if you want to," Ki said. "Find out how a master of this poking business gets the job done."

"Hell, boy, you can't teach me a thing about screwing."

"You might be surprised," Ruthie said, "Sit down, take your cock in your hand, and watch and learn."

Henshaw sat down on the other bed four feet away and glowered at them. His hand began rubbing his crotch.

Ki got up from the bed and stripped off the rest of his clothes. He dropped back on top of Ruthie and began sucking on her breasts.

"Biggest tits I've ever seen," Ki said. Ruthie growled back at him. He sucked awhile more, then spread her legs and lifted them high in the air.

"Second-story job," Ki said. He went between her legs and let them come down to his shoulders, then he spread her cheeks with his hands, to find her glory hole and slant in.

"Oh, damn, you found my cunnie right off!" Ruthie shouted. "Some guys hunt for ten minutes before they find me."

Ki watched Henshaw. He had started to sweat. His hand rubbed the bulge at his crotch harder now. His legs had spread and he was panting.

Ki pounded into Ruthie for ten strokes, then came out. "Over on your hands and knees, woman."

Ruthie played her part beautifully, Ki thought.

"Doggie? I like the doggie."

"Ruthie, I'm a big great dane about to mount you from the rear."

Ruthie went down on her arms and shoulders with her bottom sticking up in back, and Ki adjusted, then pounded into her in one swift stroke.

He heard Henshaw moaning a few feet away.

"No problem, Brock old buddy. I won't use her up. Be plenty of Ruthie for you in a few minutes. Don't go jerking yourself off over there."

Ruthie and Ki both laughed, and Henshaw stared at them in growing anger.

Then Ki settled down to business and plowed into Ruthie like a steam hammer, and in a dozen strokes he bellowed six times, rooting as deep into the woman as he could and ending it with a scream of celebration. He pushed Ruthie down on her big belly and flopped on top of her back, tired but not as exhausted as he pretended to be.

Brock Henshaw came to his feet. He marched over to the other bed, his pants bulging conspicuously. He stared down at them a minute, then poked Ki in the back.

"Hey, Ki, you Japo. My turn. Get the hell off my woman."

Ki didn't move. He waved with one hand to go away.

Henshaw poked Ki again. "Come on, bastard, my turn. My goddam turn with Ruthie."

This time Ki lifted up and rolled off the bed. He shrugged. "Hell, I guess that's up to the lady."

Ki pulled on his clothes fast. Ruthie hadn't moved from where she had collapsed on her stomach.

"Hey, bitch. Ruthie. My turn, dammit. What the hell you think I'm paying you for?"

He sat down on the bed beside her. The moment he touched her back, she rolled to the far side of the bed and jumped up. Her big breasts bounced like gunny sacks of wheat. She backed away.

"Go away, Henshaw. I don't want no more tonight. I don't want to screw you."

He stared at her. One hand formed into a fist, and he hit the mattress. "What?" he bellowed. "You promised when we came in. You're a whore, you can't say no."

"Hell I can't. I just did. Now get out of my house. Go on. Get out!"

"Can't do this. I'm tighter than a just wound clock. Come on, Ruthie, I poked you plenty of times. I need you right now."

"Get your ass out of my house. I don't want to see you no more. I'm sick of you and your sagging belly."

Henshaw stood and stared across the bed at her. Then he roared and jumped on the bed to cross it. His sudden weight knocked out the three boards that held the springs up, and the whole bed crashed to the floor. Henshaw lost his balance and went down with it.

By the time he got to his feet, Ruthie had run around the bed frame and out the door. Henshaw looked around, but Ki was gone, too.

Hell, Ruthie was just playing games with him. She really wanted his three bucks. He went to the hall and looked up and down but didn't see Ruthie sticking her fanny out a doorway as she'd done before teasing him.

He stormed from room to room, until he'd checked all six, even the kitchen. Ruthie wasn't there.

"Oh damn that whore!" Henshaw yelled. He felt it starting to come but tried to block it. The goddam voices again. He raged at them, but they came stronger and stronger. He held his head with both hands, then ran out the front door and to the street.

For three blocks he ran down the avenue that paralleled Main, then he stopped, panting hard. His erection had collapsed when his head began to hurt.

Now he bellowed a long scream. A light went on in a house near him. He walked on down the street, then turned up to

Main. Damn, he didn't have his long coat or anything. He turned and ran home, went around back quietly, got the coat from the peg on the porch, and came back outside.

He slipped on the coat and felt in the pockets. He had the six-inch knife, the small jar of kerosene, and the pliers. He frowned. For a moment he thought there was only one set of pliers there. Must be two. He checked and found just one. He must have dropped one pair somewhere. One would have to do.

The voices screamed nonstop in his brain. He had to wash them away. The only way he could do it. Animal blood didn't work anymore. He'd have to find somebody. Damn. He'd been trying not to let the voices come anymore. He wanted to study his Shakespeare. Tomorrow night. Yes.

He walked quickly to Main Street and down half a block to the first dark cross street. There were no lights nearby. A saloon up three doors. Yes, should be somebody soon. He'd do it in the alley again, no fire, just the upside-down crosses in blood, then lots of blood. He had to wash his hands and his arms this time. Lots of blood.

A man came down the boardwalk, moving quickly. He stayed at the outside, next to the street, watched the darkness of the cross street as he passed, and stepped back to the boardwalk on the other side and kept going.

No chance. Not drunk at all. He hated men who could hold their whiskey.

Henshaw waited. Another man came out of the saloon. He was so drunk he could hardly walk. He looked both ways, then went toward Henshaw.

Yes! This was the one. Henshaw could feel it. The voices beat on his brain, and he was afraid the drunk could hear them. He came slowly, weaving, staggering a little. At the cross street, he looked into the darkness, snorted, and stepped off the boardwalk to the dirt of the street not a foot from the blackness.

Henshaw tensed. He had the knife out. He'd put it to the man's throat and not cut him until later. This one was so drunk he could be subdued with a stranglehold.

The man came another step, and Henshaw lunged, grabbed

him around the throat, and put the knife next to the man's eyes.

"Say a word and I slice your eyeball in half," Henshaw growled at the man. He pulled the victim out of the faint light of the moon and the lamps across the way. When he was halfway back down the deserted street, he stopped.

"I'll take the blade away from your eyes if you promise not to scream and to keep quiet," Henshaw said. The man nodded.

Henshaw pulled the knife down, deciding on a stab in the man's side to keep him hurting and quiet. He pulled back the knife and to his surprise felt his hand caught and twisted behind his back. Then a thunderous blow hit him in the side of his neck, and he lost his hold on his victim and slumped to his knees.

In the faint light he could see a figure outlined against the lights from Main Street. The form there moved slightly, and Henshaw felt a foot slam into the side of his jaw, jolting him sideways into the dirt.

Before he could move, two men dropped on him, caught his arms and fastened them with handcuffs behind his back, and rolled him over.

A match flared. The light blinded Henshaw. All he could see were white spots in front of his eyes.

"Well, well, Mr. Henshaw, good of you to come to our little party."

Henshaw knew the voice—Sheriff Kellerman.

He coughed. "Sheriff. Glad to see you. Somebody pulled me into the dark here, tried to stab me. Don't know who it was."

"It was me, Deputy Sheriff Parnell, Mr. Henshaw. You were the one who thought I was drunk and pulled me in here at knife point. I'd say you're in a lot of trouble."

Another match flared, then a third. Then he could see Ki, that Texas woman, Starbuck, and the sheriff.

"Henshaw, I'm arresting you for three murders and this assault and attempted murder. This is going to be the easiest murder trial in the county's history. I already have the Birdman in jail, Henshaw. He's singing like a true canary, giving me all the eyewitness evidence I need for that killing of Will Stone.

One is all we need. We know that you did the other two as as well."

They hoisted Henshaw to his feet. His shoulders slumped. His hands were still tight behind him.

"Hell, I guess you caught me," Henshaw said. Then in the fraction of a second he tensed and charged forward past the three, toward the lights of Main Street.

"Don't shoot him!" Sheriff Kellerman barked.

Ki had a *shuriken* in hand, and the moment the form was silhouetted against the lights on Main Street, he threw. The eight-pointed star hit Henshaw in the left thigh and tumbled him into the dirt of the side street. He bellowed in agony. But his hands were still behind him, and he couldn't pull out the star.

The next morning, about ten o'clock, Ki and Jessie said their goodbyes to Sheriff Kellerman at the courthouse.

"You sure you have everything from us you need on the case," Jessie said.

Kellerman nodded. "With the signed statement we have from the Birdman and the evidence in the pockets of the black coat, we have Brock Henshaw wrapped up for a quick trial, and the need to build our first county gallows."

"I'm glad. I had a meeting with the mill manager this morning early. He'll get the stolen goods from the Stone barn and keep closer tabs on the supplies after this.

"I also had a report from the hard-rock mine. The men there say they don't know for sure if this is the mother lode or just a splinter of a vein that they've found. Won't know until they follow the vein by digging another hundred feet of tunnel. That'll take some time."

"The gold panners have peaked up on the Page Creek strike," Kellerman said. "We have over eighty claims up there, most of them marginal. But you know gold prospectors. They'll be working the rest of the creeks and dozens more trying to find the mother lode."

Ki shook hands with Kellerman, grinned at Jessie, and walked out of the sheriff's office.

Jessie lifted her lips to meet Mark Kellerman's, and the kiss was soft and gentle, a memory kiss.

When she came away from him, Jessie smiled. "Thank you, Sheriff Mark Kellerman. I'll always remember you. Now, we have about ten minutes to get on that stage to Boise."

As the three of them walked to the stage, Jessie asked what day this was.

"June fourteenth," Kellerman said.

"Not more than two weeks left. I promised myself I'd be there for her." Jessie looked at Ki. "Remember that roan mare with the white star on her forehead? She's due to foal on the first of July. I surely want to be back at the ranch for that. Nothing more wonderful than watching a new foal come into the world, and by the time it's an hour old, it stumbles up on those spindly little legs and starts nursing."

They were the last on board the stage, but there were only two other passengers, so they had lots of room. Jessie eased down on the travel pillow she always brought along and gave a contented sigh.

As they rattled away from Ruggins, she forgot about the list of things she had wanted to do in the Northwest while she was in Portland. Ruggins had come up. The other things could wait. One thing wouldn't wait, and that was her roan mare Star and that foal that was on the way. Jessie wanted to whip the stage horses to urge them on faster. But at last she settled back in the seat. They would be there on time. They would connect with the train as soon as they could, and then they would fly over the rails to west Texas.

Ki nodded at Jessie and put one hand on his waistband, an inch from the *shuriken* throwing stars. Then he slid into his one-eyed sleep, his body relaxed and almost asleep except for that one eye, which watched over Jessie in a way his ancestors would have been proud of. Ki sighed softly. All was well, for now.

Watch for

LONE STAR AND THE DEATH MINE

136th novel in the exciting LONE STAR series
from Jove

Coming in December!

If you enjoyed this book, subscribe now and get...

TWO FREE

A $7.00 VALUE—

If you would like to read more of the very best, most exciting, adventurous, action-packed Westerns being published today, you'll want to subscribe to True Value's Western Home Subscription Service.

Each month the editors of True Value will select the 6 very best Westerns from America's leading publishers for special readers like you. You'll be able to preview these new titles as soon as they are published, *FREE* for ten days with no obligation!

TWO FREE BOOKS

When you subscribe, we'll send you your first month's shipment of the newest and best 6 Westerns for you to preview. With your first shipment, two of these books will be yours as our introductory gift to you absolutely *FREE* (a $7.00 value), regardless of what you decide to do. If

you like them, as much as we think you will, keep all six books but pay for just 4 at the low subscriber rate of just $2.75 each. If you decide to return them, keep 2 of the titles as our gift. No obligation.

Special Subscriber Savings

When you become a True Value subscriber you'll save money several ways. First, all regular monthly selections will be billed at the low subscriber price of just $2.75 each. That's at least a savings of $4.50 each month below the publishers price. Second, there is never any shipping, handling or other hidden charges—*Free home delivery*. What's more there is no minimum number of books you must buy, you may return any selection for full credit and you can cancel your subscription at any time. A TRUE VALUE!

A special offer for people who enjoy reading the best Westerns published today.

WESTERNS!

NO OBLIGATION

Mail the coupon below

To start your subscription and receive 2 FREE WESTERNS, fill out the coupon below and mail it today. We'll send your first shipment which includes 2 FREE BOOKS as soon as we receive it.

Mail To: **True Value Home Subscription Services, Inc. P.O. Box 5235
120 Brighton Road, Clifton, New Jersey 07015-5235**

YES! I want to start reviewing the very best Westerns being published today. Send me my first shipment of 6 Westerns for me to preview FREE for 10 days. If I decide to keep them, I'll pay for just 4 of the books at the low subscriber price of $2 75 each; a total $11.00 (a $21.00 value). Then each month I'll receive the 6 newest and best Westerns to preview Free for 10 days. If I'm not satisfied I may return them within 10 days and owe nothing. Otherwise I'll be billed at the special low subscriber rate of $2.75 each; a total of $16.50 (at least a $21.00 value) and save $4.50 off the publishers price. There are never any shipping, handling or other hidden charges. I understand I am under no obligation to purchase any number of books and I can cancel my subscription at any time. no questions asked. In any case the 2 FREE books are mine to keep.

Name _____

Street Address _____ Apt. No. _____

City _____ State _____ Zip Code _____

Telephone _____

Signature _____
(if under 18 parent or guardian must sign)

Terms and prices subject to change Orders subject
to acceptance by True Value Home Subscription
Services. Inc.   11239-9

From the Creators of Longarm!

Featuring the beautiful Jessica Starbuck
and her loyal half-American half-
Japanese martial arts sidekick Ki.